Calm
BEFORE THE
STORM

by Peggy J. Herring

Bella
BOOKS

September 2000

Bella Books, Inc.
P.O. Box 201007
Ferndale, MI 48220

Printed in the United States of America on acid-free paper
First Edition

Editor: Lila Empson
Cover designer: Bonnie Liss (Phoenix Graphics)

ISBN 0-9677753-1-0   (alk. paper)

for aj

Acknowledgments

I would like to thank Frankie J. Jones for her continuous support and Martha Cabrera for the emergency brainstorming session at Red Lobster. Without you two I wouldn't have met my deadline.

I would also like to thank Joan Hedahl for sharing her expertise in such a way that even I could understand it.

A very special thanks also goes to Laurie McMillen for helping me smooth out the rough edges on the manuscript and for keeping my spirits up when it looked like there wasn't a plot in sight. You're very good at what you do!

I want to also thank Kelly Smith for giving me a new home at Bella Books. I admire her courage and foresight, and I'm happy to be a part of this new adventure.

In addition, I want to express my appreciation to my good friend and Chain Gang member Therese Szymanski for many valuable suggestions. I look forward to more of her quirkiness in the future.

And I would also like to thank Sean O'Mara for the last-minute advice and for helping me add a dose of realism here and there.

Chapter One

Colonel Marcel Robicheaux moved briskly through the Command Suite and acknowledged the call to attention with a bright "good morning" before reaching the door to her office. Having everyone in the room aware of her arrival was a formality done only once a day, and Marcel always liked having it over with as soon as possible. Military customs and courtesies were ingrained in tradition, and Marcel knew that she would miss certain aspects of it when she retired, but having her presence announced before she even had her first cup of coffee every morning would always rank at the top of her things-I-can-live-without list.

William Shook, Marcel's secretary, usually gave her enough time to get her hat and coat on the rack before coming in with the day's agenda. He was a small man and impeccably groomed, often reminding Marcel of a well-dressed jockey who had ridden his last race and had reluctantly settled into a mundane government job to pay the rent. William was efficient at keeping Marcel out of trouble and on time for meetings and appointments. She would be lost without him.

"Captain Cooper from Company B needs to see you right away," William said as he scanned an index card with notes on it. "And the General's wife called to remind you about tennis at eleven-thirty."

Marcel rolled her eyes and gave him her best bored expression. "Do whatever it takes to get me out of that."

William smiled and nodded slightly.

"Any idea what Captain Cooper wants?" Marcel asked as she sat down behind her desk.

"Adult leadership, no doubt," he replied dryly. Marcel chuckled as he continued. "There's the General's staff meeting at fourteen hundred hours and an awards ceremony at fifteen-thirty." William pulled a folder out from under his arm and placed it opened in front of her with a pen ready for her to begin signing. Marcel scribbled her name on the forms and letters wherever he pointed, and they worked their way down through the pile.

"Send Captain Cooper in as soon as she gets here," Marcel said. "Let the day begin."

Captain Heidi Cooper, a lesbian who spent a lot of time trying not to appear as such, was one of two female company commanders in the battalion. Marcel felt a sense of responsibility for all soldiers under her command, whether they were officers or enlisted personnel. Heidi had a small crush on Marcel, and she always seemed to have a reason to be in Marcel's office. Occasionally they would run together at lunch, and Heidi was quick to volunteer for anything that the battalion needed help with. Heidi was a good officer who felt comfortable with Marcel on several levels. Marcel made sure that interactions between them stayed professional and above board.

As soon as William left Marcel's office, there was a short, firm knock on the door. Marcel answered with a steady, "Come in."

Captain Cooper closed the door behind her and nervously ran her fingers through her collar-length brown hair. Heidi had a stocky build and at five-foot-five was several inches shorter than Marcel. Due to strict Army regulations, keeping fit was an occupational necessity, and Heidi constantly struggled to stay within the authorized weight standards. Her naturally rosy cheeks hinted at a hypertension problem, but she had an easygoing manner and was in excellent health. Marcel smiled as she remembered someone saying "not the sharpest knife in the drawer" when they described Captain Cooper upon her arrival at Fort Sam Houston, but so far Marcel hadn't seen anything in her behavior or actions to warrant such a remark.

"Thanks for seeing me this morning," Heidi said.

"What's the problem?" Marcel asked. "Sit down. You look like hell. What's up?"

Heidi eased into the green plastic chair in front of Marcel's desk, a chair that had been specifically chosen for its lack of comfort. Marcel's theory was that if she had nice, comfortable furniture in her office, then visitors might not leave in a timely manner. She was too busy to entertain anyone, and so far the green plastic chair was serving its purpose. However, when Marcel's mother, Roslin Robicheaux, came to see her, Roslin always insisted on sitting in Marcel's chair behind the desk, refusing to sit in anyone's dumpster reject.

Marcel gave Heidi her complete attention and noticed that

Heidi's camouflage, battle-dress uniform was starched to perfection, with creases that looked as though they might snap a sleeve in half if she weren't careful.

"How can they be so stupid?" Heidi mumbled. "Sometimes they leave me absolutely speechless."

"They?" Marcel said. "They who?"

"The *troops*. You wouldn't believe the conversation I've already had this morning."

"Enlighten me."

"Sergeant Wiley Hartman," Heidi said as she sighed heavily. "He's been in the Army seven years already. He should know better. Anyway, I get a call from National Car Rental yesterday telling me that Sergeant Hartman has had one of their rental cars for two months now and won't give it back. He owes them fourteen hundred dollars. So I get him in my office to hear his side of the story, and he tells me that he did, in fact, rent a car for a week and paid for a week. Then as it turned out he needed the car longer." Exasperated, Heidi shook her head and sighed again. "He then tells me that he can't take the car back because he owes too much money on it! Can you believe that? He *owes* too much money. I tried to explain to him that each day he *keeps* the car, he will owe even *more* money, but he doesn't seem to get it. He keeps repeating over and over again that he has to keep the car because he doesn't have fourteen hundred dollars to pay the rental-car company."

Marcel leaned forward in her chair and laced her fingers together on top of her desk. *Okay,* she thought. *This sounds simple enough. A very fixable problem.*

Marcel arched an eyebrow and asked, "So what exactly do you need me for?" She leaned back in her chair and studied Heidi for a moment. The frustration on Heidi's face told her all she needed to know then. With a solution already in mind, Marcel said, "This is what you do. You call up the rental-car agency and make arrangements for him to pay the bill off from his allotment every month. Then you send him to the finance office for official financial counseling. Just make sure everything's documented."

Heidi pursed her lips. "Hmm. I didn't think about the allotment thing."

"It's the only way they'll get their money." Marcel smiled suddenly. "How long would he have kept the car?"

"Forever! According to him, he couldn't afford to take it back. Have you ever heard of anything so stupid?"

They shared a laugh for a moment, and then Heidi said, "I'd also like to take a stripe away from him. As an NCO he's supposed to be a leader. I'm not sure this guy could lead his way out of a paper bag."

Marcel frowned. "There are more effective ways to deal with him. He's in financial trouble already. If a reduction in rank produces a smaller paycheck, how's that going to help him? He's drowning here. He needs a life preserver, and you're suggesting that we throw him an anchor. I think an official counseling statement would be more appropriate at this point." Marcel laced her fingers together again and said, "Is there anything else I can help you with?"

"Uh . . . no. Thanks. I'll take care of it." Captain Cooper closed the door behind her on her way out. As soon as the door clicked shut, the telephone on Marcel's desk rang.

"The General's wife has been holding for you on line one," William said. "She isn't taking no for an answer."

"I see," Marcel said. "Thank you." She squinted menacingly at the blinking light on the phone and wondered how she was going to get out of this.

General Harlan Wheatly's young wife, Jordan, had taken a renewed interest in Marcel at the General's annual Christmas party several months ago. To Marcel's horror, Jordan had groped her twice during the party — once on the front porch as carolers sang to the guests, and then again later that same evening when Jordan pretended to spill eggnog on the front of Marcel's uniform. Before the party was over, the General's young wife finally managed to lure Marcel into the kitchen, pin her against the pantry door, and kiss her as if the world were coming to an end.

"Anyone could come in here," Marcel remembered snarling that night as she disentangled herself from Jordan's grasp.

"I hate my life, Marcel."

"You can't make that my problem, Jordan. Why did you marry him in the first place?"

"I thought it would be different. I had no idea I'd be this bored."

Marcel quickly checked her reflection in the toaster for any signs of Jordan's lipstick and said, "I also can't be the solution to your boredom either."

"You're the only lesbian I know."

"Get real. This is the Army. Lesbians are everywhere on this post."

"So point them out to me," Jordan had said with a smile. "Other than Heidi Cooper. I know about her already."

Marcel was never quite sure just how desperate Jordan was for female companionship, but she didn't trust her in the least. Even though Marcel was a firm believer that sleeping with the boss's wife wasn't in her best interest, her options were nonetheless limited. Marcel knew that if Jordan mentioned to anyone that she was a lesbian, her career would be over immediately, and Marcel was too close to retirement to have that jeopardized. Jordan was a determined, desperate woman, and Marcel had to be smart and careful when dealing with her.

Marcel picked up the phone and said in her crisp I-don't-have-time-for-you-no-matter-who-you-are voice, "Colonel Robicheaux. This is an unsecured line. How can I help you?"

Jordan wasn't the least bit impressed. "Don't pretend you don't know who this is. Eleven-thirty today. Tennis. Remember?"

Marcel took a deep breath and vowed to be as pleasant as

she could under the circumstances. Having to discourage an attractive woman wasn't something that she had a lot of experience with.

"Good morning, Mrs. Wheatly. How are you?"

This particular tennis date, like the other three tennis dates that Jordan had arranged, had come about as a result of Jordan's clever suggestions in the presence of her husband at various social gatherings. General Wheatly liked seeing his wife active and busy, since the role of military wife still wasn't agreeing with her. Jordan was restless, and the General always seemed to be at a loss as to what to do with her.

"Just don't be late," Jordan said. She was apparently still miffed at William's earlier attempt to cancel her plans.

Against Marcel's better judgment, she resigned herself to the fact that there would be a few sets of tennis in her immediate future. She decided that she'd just have to tell Jordan again how much she disliked all this flagrant aggression . . . disliked the cheap thrill of stolen kisses behind closed doors . . . the excitement and danger of having her breasts touched in broad daylight on the tennis court. With less than six weeks to go before her retirement, Marcel didn't need that in her life now. Unsatisfied married women didn't interest her in the least, and getting out of this situation as quickly as possible, with her rank and career intact, would take all of Marcel's mental resources.

"I'll be there," Marcel said, and then added, "promptly."

"And leave that stupid beeper at the office," Jordan said. "They can do without you for an hour." Her anger was slipping away; Marcel could hear it in her voice. "I've got a nice salad and a bottle of wine chilling for later. I'll send you back very happy."

Give me a break, Marcel thought as she hung up the phone. *Six more weeks of this. Give me strength.*

~ ~ ~ ~ ~

7

The idea came to Marcel a few hours later as she went to change clothes for her tennis date. She decided against wearing her usual white shorts, white pullover shirt, and white sneakers and chose instead the gray Army sweats that had been in one of her lost, but recently found again, gym bags. The sweats were ripe and disgusting—and absolutely perfect for the occasion.

Marcel tossed her beeper, a few bucks, and her military ID card in a fanny pack and left William specific instructions to page her in an hour. She then set off running toward the General's house, which was a little over two miles from Marcel's office. She knocked on Jordan's door a while later and was met with a furious glare the moment Jordan saw her.

"Damn it, Marcel," Jordan snapped. "You're sweaty already." The rhyming words made Marcel laugh, but Jordan didn't see anything funny about it. She poked her head out the door and scanned the tree-lined street for Marcel's Miata. "Where the fuck's your car? Did you *run* over here?"

Marcel nudged her way inside the door and tried to catch her breath. Being out in the open air had unfortunately made her sweats smell less offensive. "I'll need to borrow one of your rackets. I didn't feel like carrying mine. Hurry up. Chop-chop. Let's go. Some of us don't have all day."

As Jordan went up the stairs to get another racket, Marcel reminded her that a General's wife shouldn't be saying *fuck*. She laughed as she watched Jordan toss her bouncy blond ponytail around with a shake of her head and trudge up each stair uttering the word *fuck* several times with new, intense emphasis.

Marcel was ahead forty love when her beeper finally went off, and Jordan was fuming at the interruption.

"I need to use your phone."

Jordan pointed her racket at Marcel and said, "I know what you're doing."

Marcel smiled. "I'm running your tush all over the court. That's what I'm doing. Now please take me to a phone."

The General's house was across the street from the tennis courts, and they walked there in silence. Marcel had it in mind to return William's bogus call and then jog back to work for a shower and then maybe a quick lunch at the dining facility. She liked eating Army food occasionally and enjoyed mingling with the troops. She imagined that the quality of food might improve if the boss ate there more often.

Marcel hurried up the steps to the huge wooden wraparound porch. The Wheatlys lived in what was called The Pershing House, a historical landmark at Fort Sam Houston. John J. Pershing had lived there in the twenties and Dwight and Mamie Eisenhower had lived there in the forties. It was an old and truly beautiful home. Marcel always felt a sense of awe whenever she visited.

"The phone's in here," Jordan said as she motioned toward another room to the left.

Marcel picked up the outrageously ornate receiver on the seventies-model decorator cradle phone. It looked like something from a soap opera, and Marcel wasn't even sure it was real until she heard the dial tone. She called her office number, and seconds later she felt Jordan's breasts pressing softly against her back, felt her slender hands reaching around to cup her breasts. Just as Marcel was about to intentionally step on Jordan's foot to discourage anything further, William answered the phone.

Marcel cleared her throat and moved away from the antique table where the phone was, but Jordan stayed right with her and even managed to kiss the back of her neck as she rubbed her breasts more firmly against her.

"Colonel Robicheaux," Marcel said. "Someone paged me?"

"As requested," William replied.

9

Marcel closed her eyes and willed her nipples not to harden, but she knew it was hopeless. And to make matters worse, Jordan's lips were now avidly kissing her sweaty neck and sending a wave of goose bumps scampering down her arms.

"I see," Marcel said. "Thank you. I'm on my way." She hung up the phone and let Jordan turn her around. "What do you think you're doing?"

Jordan laughed. "We both know what I'm doing, and we both know that you like it." She slid a hand under Marcel's damp shirt and smiled at what she found. "And apparently you like it a lot."

"Give me a break," Marcel said as she removed Jordan's hand. But Jordan was quick and brought Marcel's hand up and placed it on her own breast and squeezed. Jordan kissed her then, and slipped her tongue into Marcel's mouth. A jolt of heat flew through Marcel's body, and just for an instant she felt herself responding. But the alarms in her head were ringing much louder than any alarms connected elsewhere, and she abruptly broke away from her.

"You know you want to," Jordan whispered as she squeezed Marcel's hand that covered her breast. "I need you."

Marcel couldn't do it. She could see twenty years swirling down a drain because of a horny officer's wife whose idea of discretion consisted of fondling only one of her lover's breasts instead of both while out in public. Marcel knew that Jordan didn't care about anyone but herself. Jordan just wanted sex.

Marcel yanked her hand back and on her way out the door mumbled, "Mamie Eisenhower lived in this house, for crissakes."

Chapter Two

"Are you sleeping okay?" Roslin asked as she studied her daughter carefully across the table. When she didn't get an answer right away, she prodded further. "Well? Are you?"

Marcel sipped her wine and shrugged. "I'm fine."

"Meaning?"

"I sleep when I'm sleepy. You know how it is."

Roslin set her menu aside and picked up her wineglass. Holding it in both hands, she propped her elbows on the table. "How long per night these days? On an average."

"A few hours here and there. Nothing new. Stop worrying. My body let's me know when it's time to sleep." Marcel was hoping her mother would move on to another subject, but deep down she knew how unlikely that was. Insomnia had been a part of Marcel's routine for most of her life, and because of it she and her mother were both unofficial experts on sleep disorders. Roslin was forever asking the questions that she already knew the answers to but felt compelled to ask anyway, while Marcel had learned to pace herself and incorporate sleepless nights into a beneficial use of time. The subject of Marcel's sleep patterns always came up, and Marcel quite often had nothing new to report.

"I still think it's stress," Roslin said. "All that traveling we did when you were a baby, and then the pressure of school and then the Army."

"Traveling when I was a kid had nothing to do with it," Marcel said, reassuring her with a kind smile. She knew that her mother was still consumed with guilt about several decisions she had made while scratching out a living for them after Marcel's father had died. Over the years, Marcel had learned that the only thing that helped to alleviate some of her mother's guilt was to reaffirm the closeness that they shared, and to remind her that there wasn't another child in the world who had felt more loved than Marcel had when she was growing up.

"So have you decided about the antique business yet?" Roslin asked. "I'd hate to see you rush into anything. Why don't you take some time off and relax for a while?"

"Relax?" Marcel said with a smile. "What's that?"

"Do the Caribbean," Roslin suggested. "Or Europe maybe. Hell, come to Vegas with me and watch your mother work for a while. It'll be fun."

Marcel chuckled at that last suggestion. It always amazed her when she thought about how her mother made a living. Roslin Robicheaux was a gambler, a *good* gambler. Poker was her game, and in world-class gambling circles she was famous. As a result of her uncanny luck and remarkable skill, Roslin owned houses on four continents, yachts, and racehorses, as well as a fleet of expensive cars — all having been obtained in lieu of cash during various high-stake poker games. Roslin traveled and worked about fifteen days out of a month; the remainder of the time she stayed busy with various charities in the San Antonio area.

"How about it?" Roslin said. "Take some time off and come with me. Chill a little."

"If I chilled any more I'd have frostbite." Hearing her mother's laughter made Marcel smile again. "I'm okay," she assured her once more. "Things are winding down in my professional life now, so that's not a problem. And I'm more relaxed and at ease with myself now than I've been in a long time. Maybe ever." Marcel raised her glass before taking another sip. "Frostbite, I tell you."

Roslin arched a brow and said, "You're so full of it that I'm surprised your eyes are still blue."

"There you go making fun of my poker face again."

"Well, it's not nice to bullshit your mother."

Marcel parked in Cricket's driveway and got the bottle of wine out of the front seat. Amanda's car was there already, which made Marcel's heart do the tango. Her emotions ranged from excitement at the possibility of seeing Amanda again, to a sense of dread at seeing her again. Amanda was Cricket's girlfriend and a successful real estate agent. The three of them had recently been spending a lot of time together, but Marcel was thinking about putting an end to that since she'd found herself feeling attracted to Amanda lately. It was an uncomfortable situation for her, and Marcel believed that Cricket and Amanda both deserved better.

Cricket Lomax had been Marcel's best friend since seventh grade. In high school, they had become lovers and had remained so until Marcel got accepted to West Point after graduation. Over the years, their relationship developed into a warm, nurturing friendship, and there was nothing they wouldn't do for each other. Cricket was the person Marcel could call at two in the morning if she needed help with anything or just wanted to talk. They were very different people — a good mixture of personality and temperament — and were extremely devoted friends. They had been through much worse, and Marcel knew she would get through this as well.

Cricket answered the door, and Marcel smiled as she handed over the bottle of wine. "It has a cork in it, so I know it's not exactly what you're used to."

Cricket took the bottle and inspected its label. Amanda stuck her blond head around the corner of the kitchen and gave a left-handed salute.

Damn, Marcel thought as she waved to her. *No one should look that good.*

"How many more days?" Amanda asked.

"Thirty six," Marcel said. Even though her upcoming retirement from the Army was getting closer, Marcel chose not to focus on it for very long. The Army had been more than just a job or a career to her. It was a way of life and so much a part of everything about her that even now it was hard to imagine being without it.

"Is your mother planning a party?" Cricket asked.

"I hope not, but it wouldn't surprise me."

Cricket placed a tray with an assortment of cheese and crackers on the coffee table, then handed Marcel a caffeine-free Diet Coke. Amanda sat on the other end of the sofa from Marcel and tried one of Cricket's hors d'oeuvre creations.

"Have you met Marcel's mother yet?" Cricket asked Amanda. "Lord have mercy, what a fox," she said as she popped a cracker in her mouth. "Too bad you take after your father, Marcel, honey."

Amanda laughed and glanced at Marcel. "I hope you at least get some respect at work, because it looks like you aren't getting any around here."

Cricket sat down on the floor with her back resting against

Amanda's legs. "Dinner in five minutes," Cricket said. "So what's your mother-the-babe up to these days? Wow. Remember the crush I used to have on her?"

"*Used* to have?" Marcel said. "You've thought she was a babe ever since we were fifteen."

Cricket sighed at the memory. "She was a babe then, too. I only dated *you* so I could be close to your mother, you know."

Marcel laughed. "Like that was a secret."

Dinner consisted of green-bean casserole, oven-fried chicken, corn on the cob, and salad, which Cricket insisted were all Marcel's favorites. During dinner the conversation stayed light and friendly, with Marcel cleverly steering the topic away from herself and retirement and more toward Cricket and her students. Cricket was the kind of person who was often mistaken for younger because of her views about life and how it should be lived. As an eighth-grade history teacher who enjoyed what she was doing, Cricket could always be counted on for a good story or two. Her students loved her, and she took her job seriously.

"I had this one student ask me who Richard Stands was," Cricket said as she helped herself to another scoop of green bean casserole.

"Richard Stands," Marcel repeated. "So who is he? I've never heard of him either." She wanted to keep Cricket talking and give her a chance to do what she did best. Marcel reasoned that the more the conversation centered around Cricket and her zoo of a life, the less opportunity there would be for Marcel to dwell on Amanda.

Damn, Marcel thought as she stood her corncob up on end and sliced the kernels off into a neat pile. *Amanda and those incredible eyes to die for. Those adorable freckles sprinkled across her nose. And that north Texas accent that slips out when she's surprised or angry. Damn, damn, damn. Cricket, you wench, how is it possible that you found this woman first?*

Exasperated, Amanda finally asked, "So who *is* he? I've never heard of Richard Stands either."

"The guy in the Pledge of Allegiance," Cricket said as if they were both as dense as fruitcakes. "Richard Stands. You know. 'I pledge allegiance to the flag of the United States of America and to the Republic for Richard Stands.' "

Marcel and Amanda looked at each other with matching puzzled expressions before they started to laugh.

"This kid said he'd heard of the guy for years and had been reciting his name forever but didn't know who he was," Cricket said.

Marcel chuckled. "My goodness. You do have your hands full."

"So what did you tell him?" Amanda asked.

"I enjoy inquisitive teenagers," Cricket said. "I wrote the pledge on the board and explained what they'd been agreeing to all these years. Word by word. After that we had a very lively discussion about the flag. We discussed burning it and seeing it as only a symbol. They have some passionate views already. I was encouraged."

As the evening continued, Marcel was glad to see that all night only one incident had made her uncomfortable. While going into the kitchen just before dessert was served, Marcel found Amanda reaching for brandy glasses on a top shelf, her smooth, tanned legs with their perfect calf definition . . . her khaki shorts revealing just enough thigh to make Marcel's heart skip a beat. Marcel managed to retreat into the dining room and focus her attention on a basketball game on television.

Marcel and her future business partner, Carmen Morales, were sitting in Carmen's kitchen brainstorming where to locate their new antique furniture business. Carmen and Marcel had been friends ever since serving a tour in Korea together several years ago. Marcel had been the battalion commander while Carmen served as the command sergeant major. They had many things in common, including listing San Antonio as a home of record, being lesbians in the Army, and having a deep love of and appreciation for old furniture. They had spent many evenings in Marcel's office talking about what they wanted to do when they retired, and they kept going back to the exact same thing each time.

Carmen would be retiring first, but she had a few family things to tend to before she could concentrate on opening any type of business. They both recognized the workings of fate when it came to how their paths had crossed, and Marcel loved talking about opening up her own antique shop when she was finally out of the Army.

Ideas and dreams were tossed about and discussed after-hours, and then came the more focused vision of what they would do "if." As their talks continued and became more serious, Marcel and Carmen made a promise to consider going into business together at some point in the future, and from there the idea for the Antique Villa was born.

They had both been making individual arrangements to be reassigned to Fort Sam Houston in San Antonio, Texas, for their last tour of duty in the Army. With Fort Sam being the Army's only training center for all medical personnel, getting an assignment there had never been a problem as long as it was applied for early enough. Carmen had started her Army career as a combat medic, while Marcel's area of expertise had been medical supply and logistics. Marcel had been assigned to Fort Sam twice already, and slots for her job title and rank were always open. Carmen's options had been a bit more limited, but she had also found a slot and eventually retired in the San Antonio area.

With carpentry and woodworking as hobbies, Carmen supplied the furniture expertise to the adventure that she and Marcel were pursuing, while Marcel had a large portion of the capital and an avid interest in shopping for and purchasing old furniture. Separately the two of them had expensive hobbies, but together they hoped to be incredibly successful in the world of antiques. They had been carefully planning this venture for almost eighteen months now, and they were ready to start devoting some serious time to it.

As far as location was concerned, Carmen had her mind set on one of the yuppie areas near downtown San Antonio; Marcel wanted to explore something outside of town on the interstate.

"What we make in profit," Carmen reminded her, "we'll end up spending on gas just to get there."

Marcel eventually relented and was willing to consider Carmen's yuppie idea, but she insisted on finding a place with adequate parking. And in Yuppieville — Anywhere, USA — parking was virtually nonexistent.

"Let's spend the weekend driving around and checking things out," Marcel suggested. "I need to get a feel for whatever neighborhood we decide on. It needs to *feel* right, you know?"

Carmen set a steaming bowl of menudo down in front of her and topped off their coffee mugs with the last of a nice decaf French Roast. Marcel loved watching Carmen putter around in the kitchen. Carmen's entire house always had such a warm, homey smell, like cookies fresh from the oven or soup simmering on a back burner. If you were in Carmen's house for very long, you'd better be prepared to eat something.

"I've got a few places in mind," Carmen said. "Should we go together or do our own thing and compare notes later?"

"Do our own thing first," Marcel said. She stirred the concoction in her bowl and blew on its contents. Carmen was across the table from her, engrossed in her own steaming bowl. Seeing Carmen in a worn flannel shirt with the sleeves rolled up made Marcel smile. Carmen always looked comfortable in her clothes no matter what she wore. Never one to move quickly or make a hasty decision, Carmen Morales was the most sensible person Marcel had ever known.

Going into business with her sounded better and better every day, and Marcel was looking forward to it.

"Can I ask you something?" Marcel said. She had recently noticed how she'd been getting sentimental about certain things lately. After twenty years in the Army and four years before that at West Point, Marcel wasn't sure how easy the transition into civilian life would be. Military traditions and responsibilities were such a big part of her, and Marcel loved her job and she loved the Army. She had given over half of her life to it, and all of that was about to end.

"You know you can ask me anything," Carmen said, noting her seriousness.

Marcel shrugged, a little embarrassed by the emotion she felt. "You were in a lot longer than me." She stirred her menudo and pretended to be interested in it. "How hard was it at first, once you retired. How much did you miss it?"

"I still miss it," Carmen said. "And it's *very* hard in the beginning." She laughed. "I still get up in the mornings and realize that I have to decide what to wear. In the Army I never had that problem."

They laughed and became pensive again. Carmen continued. "But the difference for me was finally having the freedom to be who I really am for the first time in my life."

Marcel nodded. She understood completely.

"Beginning a lesbian in the military," Carmen said, "especially one like me who couldn't hide it if I tried, is not an easy thing. I had to put up with a lot, and I've experienced the discrimination and hatred of a straight, white man's Army. But I never blamed any of that on the Army." Carmen smiled. "I loved it and I'd do it all over again. I think you feel the same way."

"Yes," Marcel said. "I do."

"But retirement brings with it a freedom from oppression. A sense of release from all the nonsense that went with it, and

19

that's what I remember now. I gave it all I had, and it was good to me. So to answer your question about do I miss it or not, my answer is yes and no. But mostly no."

They laughed together again and resumed eating. Marcel hoped to have similar feelings when her time finally came.

Late Sunday morning, they were back in Carmen's kitchen to compare notes on what they'd found during the week. As they chattered away, Marcel watched Carmen's hands work at the soft little white ball until a tortilla appeared in front of her eyes. Carmen tossed it on the grill and stirred something in a steaming pan. Carmen told her one time that when she was growing up it had been her job to make the tortillas for the family before each meal. She had seven brothers and four sisters — all still living in San Antonio.

"My brothers would select a tortilla and hold it up so the others could guess which state it was," Marcel remembered Carmen saying. Marcel laughed as she inspected the last tortilla placed on the plate, noting how it resembled Colorado in a strange way.

"So whatcha got?" Carmen asked as she poured fresh decaf coffee into their mugs and then set the chorizo-and-egg concoction down in the center of the table. "I hope you've done better than I did. I found some nice locations, but there's no parking. And I agree with you on the importance of parking."

Marcel shrugged. Her search for a satisfactory location near the interstate hadn't produced any favorable results either. But it was still too early.

"We'll keep looking," Marcel said. "I don't want to rush into anything."

~ ~ ~ ~ ~

Later that same afternoon, Marcel was home alone and enjoying the peace and quiet. Her mother was in Munich for several days either making a lot of money or else signing over the deed to some exotic mansion somewhere. Marcel often wondered when her mother would get tired of the traveling and the challenge of staying competitive. Roslin seemed quite capable of taking care of herself and always landed on her feet, but she wasn't getting any younger.

The telephone rang, and against Marcel's better judgment, she answered it. If it turned out to be the battalion CQ, then it would mean one of her troops was in trouble, most likely in jail. And if it was anyone else, then she'd almost consider it a blessing.

"Hey, you're home," Cricket said. "I never expect a live voice when I call someone anymore."

"You've reached a live person here. What's up?"

"Dinner," Cricket said. "We hardly ever see you these days."

Marcel wasn't sure what excuse to use this time. She didn't want to spend another Sunday afternoon being careful about what she said or where her eyes might tend to linger. Being around Amanda was getting harder and harder, and Marcel didn't feel like being on guard today.

"Maybe some other time," Marcel said. "My mother might be calling from Munich, and I've missed one call from her already."

"Munich," Cricket said with a sigh. "You know that's always been one of my fantasies — to be kept by your mother and travel all over the world as her sex slave."

"I'll be sure to pass that along to her."

"So how about we come over there?" Cricket said. "We'll bring the fajitas and beer. You can still sit by the phone, and we can play cards or something."

Just from the tone of her voice, Marcel could picture

Cricket with a hand on her hip and ready to start in on a lecture.

"You've bugged out on us the last three times we've invited you somewhere," Cricket reminded her. "What's up with that? Was it something I said? Something I *didn't* say? What, what, what?"

Marcel rolled her eyes. She should've known. "I've got the beer and the cards. You can bring the fajitas."

Chapter Three

Marcel answered the door and let Cricket and Amanda in. Cricket shifted a cumbersome Taco Cabana bag into her other arm and gave Marcel a hug. Amanda smiled and handed over a box from a popular bakery.

"My word," Amanda said. "What a beautiful house." Her eyes sparkled as she slowly turned in the foyer. "I had no idea you lived here. I've admired this place since I was a kid."

"Really?" Marcel said. "My mother acquired it about three years ago. It's so big that she's afraid to stay here alone." She led the way to the formal dining room where the lighting was better. "I learned very young to never completely unpack when I'm living with my mother," Marcel said. "Her next phone call could be centered around telling me we've got twenty-four hours to move."

"You're kidding, right?" Amanda said.

A few months ago, Marcel would have enjoyed teasing her, but it didn't feel right any longer. Every word Marcel uttered in Amanda's presence suddenly seemed like flirting.

"I wish I were," Marcel said. "My things stay in boxes with little wheels on them. Comes with the territory." She began setting the table and didn't realize how hungry she was until Cricket opened the carton of fajitas and filled the room with that rich, savory aroma.

"Why don't you get your own house?" Cricket asked. "With the kind of money you have, you could've been unpacked and settled years ago." She scooped up some guacamole and spread it on her taco.

"You just never know in this business," Marcel said. "I could've been on my way to Bosnia at a moment's notice. Those days weren't exactly fun. But now that I've decided to retire, I plan to become a more solid citizen. With lesbian roots and everything." She glanced around the room at the dark trim along the high white ceiling. The house had many fine, elegant features. "I'm not sure I could get my mother to leave this place though. She likes it here, and she likes the idea of my being with her."

"If you get your own place, just make sure it's big enough for the two of you," Cricket said reasonably. "I can't imagine such an arrangement with *my* mother, but yours is great. I could live anywhere with your mother. Easy."

"My mother doesn't want to live with me," Marcel said. "She wants *me* living with *her*. It's a parent-child thing. This is her way of making up for the lousy childhood she thinks she gave me."

Cricket raised an eyebrow. "Try that one again. You had a great childhood. You traveled all over the world. You were by her side every minute of every day until you were twelve years old. You were more like sisters than anything else. Every child should feel so loved."

Marcel smiled. "You and I know that, but when I tell her such things she never believes me. She prefers to remember the nights a few years later when she had to call me and say, 'Sorry, baby. I lost the Ponderosa.' That was always my cue to start packing up our belongings. We'd be moving."

Cricket chuckled. "And they'd move from one nice place to another nice place. Never a dump. Always moving up, up, up."

Amanda shook her head. "I don't get it. Why would she gamble away your home?"

Marcel glanced around the enormous room with its antique furnishings and priceless art — the Monet on the far wall set off by cleverly placed track lighting and the antique French cherry armoire from the Louis Philippe period.

"I think it's a tax thing," Marcel said delicately. "My mother has an aversion to paying them. I don't ask and she doesn't tell, but I'm under the impression that the IRS doesn't know she exists. It's a complicated issue and something we seldom discuss."

"I've always thought of your mother as some kind of spy or something," Cricket said with a twinkle in her eye. "Deep into international intrigue."

"Hardly," Marcel said. She remembered how her mother used to tease her about being such a little patriot. They had spent many nights discussing ethics and moral behavior, and debating the evils of the Internal Revenue Service. Roslin believed that any tax on one's income was an illegal tax and didn't have to be paid. Roslin's association with one particular group of gamblers had reshaped her philosophy about money several years ago. Roslin shared her winnings with no one — especially a government that spent taxpayers' money so frivolously. Marcel had heard the arguments scores of times over the years and had finally learned to accept her mother's position and move on. They had agreed to disagree. Marcel paid taxes. Her mother didn't. Marcel got the impression once that her mother had even denounced her American citizenship in some sort of official capacity, but it was never confirmed. That was another issue they didn't discuss.

"Oh," Cricket said. "Speaking of that don't-ask-don't-tell nonsense, when is your retirement ceremony? Don't they have a parade or something formal for you?"

"Yes," Marcel said. "A change-of-command ceremony and then a retirement ceremony. It's really no big deal, but you're both invited, of course. Invitations aren't necessary."

"I remember when you graduated from West Point," Cricket said as she swooned and clutched her chest. "All those women in uniform. Lord have mercy!"

"Oh please," Marcel said.

"I flew up there with her mother," Cricket explained excitedly as she reached over and grabbed Amanda's hand. "It was like a double dose of heaven. West Point women and sharing a room with her mother in a cozy hotel."

Marcel could feel that dreaded sinking sensation rushing through her again at just seeing Cricket and Amanda touch. She hated feeling this way — absolutely hated it.

"Yes, yes, yes. All those women *and* Roslin," Cricket said dramatically as she fanned herself with a limp tortilla.

Amanda snatched her hand back away from her. "I never realized you had such a thing for older women."

"Not all older women," Cricket informed her. "Just this one. I dream about her and fantasize about her all the time. Always have and always will! And you needn't worry, darling. Roslin thinks I'm a bozo."

Marcel laughed. "You are a bozo, but that's neither here nor there." She went to the kitchen to get them more beer and returned to find her guests playfully feeding each other fajita morsels. *Jesus, it's gonna be a long night,* Marcel thought wearily. It occurred to her then to maybe drink more than she had originally intended to that evening, but she decided against it. Marcel had never been one to cry in her beer, and she refused to start now. She was determined to get past the infatuation she had with Amanda. Lately a large amount of energy had been spent on keeping her hormones and irritation under control. Dyke drama was something she wasn't accustomed to dealing with.

As the evening continued, they played hearts and discussed a wide array of subjects that eventually included the Civil War, the Australian Open, and the latest movie getting panned by the critics. When Roslin finally called at eleven-thirty, Marcel, Amanda, and Cricket had just finished partaking of cheesecake and decaf coffee and were almost ready to call it a night. Marcel could tell by the sound of her mother's voice on the phone that she had done well during this trip. Roslin had what Marcel liked to refer to as her "three-glass" voice, where, after three glasses of wine, she would become a bit more animated than usual.

"You weren't sleeping, were you?" Roslin asked, always her first question whenever Marcel answered the phone.

"Of course not. You know better. Cricket and Amanda are here keeping me company."

"I see," Roslin said with mock severity. "How many times have I told you, young lady, no wild parties in the house while your mother is away." Roslin cut loose with her three-glass laugh.

Marcel chuckled and shook her head as she remembered that line from her hectic high school days. Her mother's memory and ability to retrieve even the most trivial information never failed to surprise her.

"So things are going well?" Marcel asked. "I won't have to change my name or anything?"

"It's been a while since things were that bad."

"Hold on. Cricket wants to talk to you." Marcel handed the phone to Cricket, who was waving her hands for her chance at the phone.

"You're an amazing woman," Amanda said suddenly. "Has anyone ever told you that?"

Startled, Marcel looked at Amanda for the first time all evening. She had earlier made it a point not to do so since she imagined that her thoughts and desires could be reflected in her eyes.

"Uh . . . no," Marcel said, answering Amanda's question. "What makes you think so?"

"Your confidence and the way you don't take yourself too seriously." Amanda tidied up by collecting napkins, plates, and silverware. "Cricket adores you. It used to make me jealous until I realized how silly it was."

"You're right," Marcel said as she began helping with the cleanup effort. This was the longest conversation they'd had in weeks, and already she was enjoying it too much. "Being jealous of me *is* silly. Cricket and I haven't been lovers in months."

"*Months*?" Amanda gasped as she dropped a fork on an empty plate. The noise seemed to bounce off the walls and echo down the long hallway. "Did you say *months*?"

Marcel laughed. "I'm teasing you."

"I think I need another drink," Amanda said as she collapsed in her chair, picked up a stale tortilla, and playfully began fanning herself with it.

"Really," Marcel said as she silently chastised herself for wanting to prolong the banter. "It's been twenty-five years if it's been a day for us. Cricket and I were curious bumbling teenagers together. Lucky to escape with our friendship intact."

Fingers snapping across the room caught their attention as Cricket held up the phone and said, "I'm through flirting with your mother. Now she wants to talk to you again for some reason."

"Imagine that," Marcel said as she took the phone back.

Cricket kissed her on the cheek. "It's late. We'll let ourselves out. I'll call you tomorrow."

Marcel watched them gather their things and wave. Amanda's smile sent a little surge of energy zipping through

Marcel's heart. *I have to stop seeing so much of them,* she thought again for the twentieth time. *I have to.*

Initially it seemed like just another ordinary day, but in reality this one was very different from any other in Marcel's life. Marcel had gotten three hours of uninterrupted sleep the night before, which made her feel rested and refreshed. She was ready, and felt as though she'd waited her whole life for this.

The weather was promising to cooperate for the outdoor ceremony later that afternoon, and everything appeared to be going well. She added the finishing touches to her impressive uniform as it hung from the closet door in her room. The time for true sentiment had arrived, and even though Marcel tried shooing it away without another thought, her eyes still misted over occasionally. She'd given the Army the best years of her life. The sacrifices had been numerous, but so had the rewards, and she was ready to close this chapter of her life and begin something new.

Roslin got up early as well, and the two of them had coffee and toast together. Marcel knew that her mother could tell she'd been crying already. Marcel wanted to get the majority of this emotional upheaval out of her system before she had to go to work and put on her colonel's face one last time.

"Never in a million years would I have thought you'd stay in for twenty," Roslin said in amazement.

Marcel shrugged. "That was never my intention, of course, but the promotions were always there and good assignments outnumbered the bad ones." With a smile she added, "And the next thing I knew I had too many years invested to get out."

"Any regrets?"

"A few."

"Some I know of." Roslin got up and kissed her daughter on top of the head. "You look very intimidating in uniform, my sweet. You'll miss that. I know this is hard on you, but you'll be fine."

"I know." Talking about it was threatening to upset her. "I just need to stay busy."

That afternoon there was a luncheon for her where General Wheatly spoke eloquently in Marcel's behalf. Roslin was there too, delighting Marcel's coworkers with her unending tales of adventure from all parts of the world. Roslin loved being around people in the military; travel was just one of many things she had in common with them. She had either been through, to, or close to almost any city where they could've been born, and she had been in a poker game in every corner of the world where any one of them could've been stationed. Roslin was charming and personable, and had passed on that particular trait to her daughter. Mother and daughter had a sense of presence about them — a stateliness with smooth, delightful edges. They looked nothing alike, but they had similar mannerisms and keen senses of humor. Along with Cricket Lomax, Marcel considered her mother to be a dear friend and confidant.

Jordan Wheatly, General Wheatly's young tennis-playing wife, was there at the luncheon too, sitting on the other side of Marcel. Jordan made sure their elbows constantly touched and that Marcel's thigh was adequately appreciated each time Jordan rearranged her napkin in her lap. Marcel didn't want to make a scene, so she pretended to ignore her while carrying on conversations all around them, but Jordan seemed to become more bold as time went on. She leaned over and whispered outlandish, suggestive things in her ear and enjoyed seeing the flash of anger in Marcel's eyes.

"What are you saving it for?" Jordan whispered. "Or should I say *who* are you saving it for?"

"Please keep your hands to yourself," Marcel said through

clenched teeth. *But after the Christmas party fiasco,* she thought, *why should anything this woman does surprise me?*

"You kissed me back after tennis the other day," Jordan whispered with a smirk. "Those lips don't lie. You want it as much as I do."

"You're a beautiful woman, Jordan," Marcel whispered in return, "but you're also one of the most selfish people I've ever known."

"Is that what you think of me?"

"Sex is the only thing that interests you, and you don't care who you hurt when you're trying to get it."

"You're wrong there. I've wanted you for a long time. If you hadn't been so worried about your precious career, we could've had some good times together."

For emphasis she rubbed Marcel's thigh again and pushed Marcel's skirt up a little, and had it not been for the long tablecloths, the entire restaurant would have known what was going on. Marcel selected a silverware piece and from under the table gave the back of Jordan's hand a nice whack. The yelp that followed made Marcel feel vindicated for the time being, but after a few minutes Jordan leaned over and whispered, "I knew you'd get around to forking me sooner or later."

Marcel slowly shook her head and tried not to smile, but they both ended up laughing. Marcel again tried to concentrate on the other conversations around her, but the little minx beside her still wasn't finished.

"There's something about you, Marcel," Jordan whispered. "I don't know what it is, but it makes me want to tease you until you squirm. Until you lose control and finally submit. By the way, Big Boy's leaving for Panama tomorrow. We could get a lot done while he's gone."

There were times when Jordan reminded Marcel of a gangster's girlfriend — very sexy and more than able to get just about anything she wanted. She had little nicknames for certain people and often called her husband "Big Boy" when he wasn't around. Once Marcel even heard her refer to the General's aide as "Buffalo Butt." Jordan was smart and knew how to use her femininity to her advantage. Marcel thought of her as the most clever and dangerous person she knew. Smacking the General's wife or defending herself with an array of restaurant utensils wasn't productive, and Marcel knew that. She did consider, however, since Jordan liked attention so much, that maybe ignoring her would be the smartest thing to do. It was obvious that Marcel couldn't complain about her to anyone, and Jordan used that to her advantage as well. Marcel felt fortunate to have survived Jordan's rapt attention as long as she had under the circumstances, but all of that was nearly over now. After today there was nothing Jordan could do to hurt her career any longer. Marcel would finally be free from all the games and confrontations.

Having finally reached her limit with the verbal innuendoes and thigh touching, Marcel abruptly moved her chair back and set out to mingle with her luncheon guests while they ate. She went from table to table, talking with them and thanking everyone for coming. Several asked about her plans after retirement.

"Antiques," she said, smiling engagingly. "Buying and selling. I don't have any business cards yet because we don't have a building, but get ready for our grand opening coming up soon."

Much later, after everyone had finished their lunch and the chattering had begun again, Marcel was given the Legion of Merit award and had to endure a mini-roast from various department chiefs in the command. She was well liked, and Marcel's reputation as a fair and dynamic leader was evident in their remarks. When it was Marcel's turn to address the group, she swallowed hard and forced the lump in her throat back into place. She was determined not to cry, and she didn't.

Her voice, however, took on a husky quality during her parting words.

Roslin, Cricket, Amanda, and Carmen came toward the end of the day for Marcel's change of command ceremony, a formality where Marcel actually relinquished the command of the battalion to her replacement. The troops, in formation by company, sweltered in the heat even though a nice breeze was blowing. After that came the retirement ceremony where Marcel and three other officers were honored. The Army band played its brassy tunes while medals were presented and given out and hands were shook.

Marcel met up with her friends and family afterward and teased her mother about crying. Marcel herself had felt that lump return to her throat more than once during the band's rendition of "Stars and Stripes Forever." It was a relief to have the formalities over with, and even though Marcel had been there every step of the way, none of it seemed real to her yet.

"Who's the blond babe that keeps checking you out?" Cricket whispered as she nodded toward Jordan. "She hasn't taken her eyes off you the entire time we've been here."

"I noticed that too," Amanda said.

"You're both being silly. That's Jordan Wheatly. The General's wife."

Cricket let out a gasp and then tugged on Marcel's sleeve excitedly. "You mean the one who cornered you in the kitchen at Christmas? The one who leaves little love notes under your windshield wiper? Omigod! Are you nuts? Why are you dodging this woman?"

Marcel cringed at each reminder. She had forgotten that she had told Cricket about the Christmas kiss and the notes. Seeing her discomfort, Cricket said, "Oh, Marcel, honey. You've gotta loosen up, girl. There's a great big lesbian world out there just waitin' for you!"

"I'm as loose as I plan to get for a while."

Cricket laughed. "Then at least introduce us to her. She's hungry for . . . for companionship, I'm sure. Which one of those old farts is the General?"

Amanda and Marcel looked at her in utter disbelief, but before the festivities were concluded, Jordan Wheatly was well acquainted with everyone.

Chapter Four

Much to Marcel's initial dismay, Roslin had invited nearly eighty people to a reception at the Four Seasons Hotel downtown on the Riverwalk to celebrate her retirement. Marcel hated surprises and had known nothing about the party, but the enthusiasm of the guests made her brief annoyance short-lived.

There was a long, brightly decorated table with a fine selection of hors d'oeuvres and a fully functioning bar for the guests. The party was located out on a breezeway where the trickling of a small waterfall from the river below added enough atmosphere to make the setting tropical in nature and very relaxing.

Music spilled out from the hotel's lounge close by, and

Marcel could see Cricket, Amanda, and another woman near the buffet table deep in conversation with Roslin. Marcel knew she was staring, but couldn't stop herself from wanting her and aching with desire each time Amanda came into focus. Marcel often wondered if Cricket knew how incredibly lucky she was. Cricket had a tendency to bore easily, but she'd been with Amanda longer than she'd been with most of her other lovers, and Marcel could easily see Amanda as the perfect woman for Cricket.

Someone brushed up against Marcel, and she felt the presence of a firm breast pressing into her arm. Jordan then leaned closer to whisper, "Interested in getting a room for later?" The perfume gave her away much more quickly than the breast had. "I took Big Boy to the airport," Jordan said in a low, throaty voice. "That gives us the weekend." Her smile was confident and flirtatious, and it was evident that she liked what she was doing.

"Why do you waste all of this on me?" Marcel asked simply. "I'm not interested."

"This isn't about you, Marcel. This is about me." Jordan smiled again and touched her top lip with her tongue. "I like being good to me, and I think you're exactly what I need."

"And it was so silly of me to think of you as selfish."

Jordan threw her head back and laughed. "I love teasing you. I think your indifference to my endearing personality is what makes me want you so much. If you would just give in a few times, I'd get you out of my system."

Up until then, Marcel had never quite understood what Jordan saw in her or where Jordan had initially gotten the impression that Marcel would be even remotely interested in sleeping with her. Now it made a little more sense.

They had been stationed in Germany together about five years ago. Jordan was a first lieutenant in the Army Nurse

Corps at the same hospital where Marcel was the comptroller. Other than the fact that Marcel was single and not actively pursuing the male gender, Jordan had no way of knowing for sure whether or not Marcel was a lesbian. Marcel had impeccable military bearing and a no-nonsense attitude about her work; her appearance and conduct gave nothing away. Only a handful of people knew for sure about Marcel's sexual persuasion, and it was imperative to her career that things remain that way.

Jordan, however, seemed to always like a challenge. Marcel had seen her with several members of the women's softball team on two occasions, and at another time she had seen her out dancing with a group of male paratroopers fresh from a training exercise. It was obvious that Jordan liked holding both ends of the rope, and that alone was enough to convince Marcel that she didn't want anything to do with her.

Jordan's early interest in Marcel came about through a confrontation in the hospital parking lot while they were in Germany. Marcel got to work early one morning and found a car in her reserved parking space. Marcel parked behind the car, blocking it in, and then called the military police so a ticket could be issued before they towed the car away. Needless to say, Jordan was unhappy when she came out to find them hoisting her car up in the air. She tried for five minutes to talk the MP out of a ticket, but only succeeded in angering him even though he agreed not to have her car towed away.

After that incident, Jordan smirked a lot whenever she met Marcel in the hallway, and she would occasionally call her up with bogus hospital budget problems just to keep in touch. Marcel never quite trusted her. Hanging out in crowded elevators seemed to be one of Jordan's favorite pastimes, and one day in a full elevator Jordan positioned herself behind Marcel while she proceeded to rub Marcel's butt in a slow, deliberate fashion. There was no place to go and no way to move. Marcel turned her head and gave her a get-your-hands-off-my-ass look, which Jordan answered with a sweet smile and a silent air kiss.

All of this predated the Department of Defense's policy on sexual harassment, but Marcel had ways of her own to handle such behavior, a few of which included taking the stairs instead of an elevator, having her secretary screen all of her calls, and, even more effective, consuming garlic. Not long after that, Colonel Wheatly assumed command of the hospital.

Colonel Harlan Wheatly was an orthopedic surgeon on the fast track to general. His wife of twenty years had died two years prior to his new assignment, and he arrived in Germany with his grief finally beginning to relinquish its hold on him. Colonel Wheatly and Jordan dated and then less than six months later got married. Jordan left the Army, gave up her nursing career, and seemed to enjoy her new role as a military doctor's wife. Marcel was hard pressed to believe that Jordan had changed much, and her theory was proven correct one day at an intramural tennis event.

Marcel was changing clothes after her tennis match and heard the door to the locker room open. Jordan came in and proceeded to make her move. She kissed Marcel and had a hand on her right breast before Marcel could even express her shock. Instead of kissing her back, Marcel knocked her hand away and said, "What the hell are you doing?" while Jordan's lips tried to cover hers again.

"Just trying to be friendly."

"Anyone could come in here!"

"So that's the problem?" Jordan said with a winning smile. "The lack of privacy?"

"I see that getting married didn't change you much. If anything, it's made you bolder."

"Some things are just irresistible." Jordan placed her thin, manicured index finger gently under Marcel's chin and made Marcel look at her. "I'm very attracted to you," she said simply. "And I know you're a lesbian."

"How do you know that?" Marcel asked as she reached for her shirt on the wooden bench and quickly put it on.

Jordan smiled again and said, "A hunch. And a lot of wishful thinking. So how about it?"

"I'm sorry, but that's impossible."

Jordan tossed her blond head back and laughed. "You're about to hurt my feelings."

"I'm not interested."

Jordan touched Marcel's chin once more and said, "I'm sure I could change your mind."

As Marcel gathered up her things, she repeated again that she wasn't interested. "I won't jeopardize my career for a fling with my boss's wife. No matter how good you look or how lonely you are." Marcel finished buttoning her shirt. "There are dozens of lesbians in this hospital who would be very happy to —"

"I don't want them. I want you."

Marcel shrugged and stuffed her clothes in her gym bag. "You need to reconsider your options."

Marcel spent the rest of her assignment in Germany dodging Jordan and became very good at it. Marcel had heard a few weeks later that Jordan and the new department of nursing chief were an item, and Marcel reasoned that if she herself had heard about it, then it probably wouldn't be long before Colonel Wheatly knew about it too.

From Germany Marcel was sent to Korea to fulfill her short-tour obligation, and then twelve months later was assigned back to Fort Sam Houston, Texas. It was Marcel's third tour at Fort Sam, which she considered home, and because of her medical service corps training, it was an easy place to get assigned to. She had been back only a year, however, when the Wheatlys arrived, and Colonel Wheatly was now General Wheatly and the new commander of the hospital at Fort Sam Houston.

~ ~ ~ ~ ~

"You need another drink," Marcel heard her mother say as she handed her a glass of wine. Roslin was beaming at having surprised her with a party.

"No kidding."

"So how does it feel to be retired?"

"I was wondering the same thing. It's only been a few hours, but so far so good." She sighed. "I'll probably know more tomorrow when I have no meetings to attend, no papers to sign, no young careers to shape and mold."

"Oh, baby. You'll be okay."

Marcel sipped her wine and smiled as her mother hugged her. "How does it feel to have a daughter old enough to be retired?"

"Ouch!"

Marcel laughed and gave her an extra squeeze. "It's a wonderful party. Thank you."

"Carmen, William, and Cricket did most of the work. I just came up with the idea and signed the check." Roslin leaned a bit closer and whispered, "So. Is it true that the General's wife leaves love notes on your car?"

Marcel scanned the crowd in search of Cricket. She found her with Carmen and an unidentified dark-headed woman near a gurgling fountain.

"Well, is it?" Roslin asked.

"Yes, it's true."

"Why didn't you tell me about this before?"

"I kept hoping it would go away." Marcel continued searching the crowd; she finally saw Amanda on the other side of the breezeway talking with a small group of people. And it didn't surprise her in the least to find Jordan in the middle, vying for attention.

The next morning, Marcel and Roslin were both slow in moving around. Marcel's retirement celebration had extended well into the wee hours of the morning and had left her feeling tired and groggy.

Roslin made coffee and cinnamon toast for them, and they sat around the breakfast nook yawning and stretching.

"So this is it," Roslin said, indicating Marcel's robe and slippers. "This is what retirement looks like?"

Marcel glanced down at her robe. "Must be."

"And you don't even care what time it is, do you?"

"I shouldn't. No." She looked over at the clock on the microwave. *Morning report and the weekly budget meeting are over with already. Nope. Don't miss any of that at all.*

"Great party last night," Marcel said. "I heard several people say so. Must've cost you a bundle."

"Worth every cent. How often will my only child retire from something? I'm just glad I lived to see it."

Marcel laughed. "You talk like you're ancient. Are you going with me today?"

"Are you still doing that thrift shop thing? Those places always smell so funky."

After breakfast they loaded up the backseat and the trunk of Marcel's BMW with twenty year's worth of military uniforms and accessories. Marcel had spent what was left of the morning reining in her emotions, and having her mother with her was making it all easier. Once they arrived at the thrift shop on post, Roslin was less enthusiastic about helping.

"If it smells anything like I remember, I'm not going in," Roslin warned with a crinkled nose.

Marcel arched an eyebrow as she lay her dress blue uniform across her mother's outstretched arms. "How many of these places have you ever been in?"

"My Aunt Hattie used to drag me to thrift shops all the time when I was a kid," Roslin said, "and they embarrassed the hell out of me. What would I have done if my friends had seen me there?" She laughed and gave a playful grunt as Marcel piled more uniforms on. "We got some good bargains back then though."

She's right, Marcel thought as she made her way through the door to the thrift shop on post. *It does smell a little funky in here.* Having her mother with her made the whole process more fun and less traumatic. To Marcel these uniforms weren't just clothes she had worn. This small mountain of green fabric represented her entire military career. It didn't surprise her that she felt emotional, and she wondered how long the transition would take. *Just stay busy,* she thought. *And that shouldn't be a problem! I've got lots to do!*

By the time the paperwork was signed and Marcel was ready to go, Roslin had gone shopping and found a nice reading lamp that she wanted.

"If Aunt Hattie could only see me now," she said with a wink.

"Ever been to a lesbian bookstore?" Marcel asked her mother when they finally got back in the car.

Roslin's what-do-you-think look made them both laugh.

"Then we're about to broaden your horizons."

At the bookstore a while later, Marcel was having trouble deciding which rainbow sticker she wanted to put on her car. There were about thirty different kinds to choose from. She'd waited years for this moment, and in a way considered this particular purchase as her official coming out. As she touched each sticker, Marcel knew exactly what Carmen had been talking about. *It's not just the symbols,* she thought. *Not just a label to buy and put somewhere for the world to see. It's the freedom to be here in this place and the knowing that who I am is no longer something to hide.*

"People don't usually put bumper stickers on a Beemer, hon," Roslin informed her.

"This isn't just any bumper sticker, Mom. This is my life. The new me. As Carmen says, I'm finally free from oppression and Uncle Sam's tyranny."

Roslin shrugged. "In that case get two." She picked up the rainbow sticker shaped like the state of Texas. "I like this one. You'd better get one for the Miata, too. You can't be driving heterosexual vehicles around now that you're officially gay."

The cute little butch clerk behind the counter pointed to the rack of displayed rainbow stickers and said, "I had a straight lady come in here once and she bought one of each to put on her car. She said it kept her teenagers from driving it."

Fifteen minutes later, Marcel had made up her mind about which stickers she wanted, and much to Marcel's surprise her mother had found several things in the store to buy as well.

"I have a question," Roslin said after a moment. "What exactly is the point of doing this? Of identifying your car in such a way? What if a bunch of bubbas found you somewhere and recognized that sticker for what it is? Aren't you asking for trouble?"

"A lot of *gay* people don't know what these stickers mean," Marcel said. "It's important that gays and lesbians recognize each other when we're out and about. I don't want anyone assuming I'm straight."

"Next you'll be wanting a tattoo," Roslin mumbled good-naturedly.

"You've got me beat with that one, now don't you?"

"A stupid dare from my college days."

"What are you buying, by the way?"

Roslin held up a puzzle of two nude men in an embrace. "If Aunt Hattie could only see me now."

Cricket called at about ten-thirty one evening a few days later just to talk. Marcel and Carmen had spent most of the day looking for a place to lease for the business. Marcel was tired but not sleepy. Sometimes she wondered if she would ever have a decent night's sleep again.

43

"There's this teacher at school who is really hot," Cricket said.

Marcel stretched out on the sofa in the living room with her cordless phone. "Oh?"

"We've been eating lunch together at school. I'm thinking about asking her out."

Confused, Marcel slowly sat up and said, "You're what?"

"She's really cute. She teaches seventh-grade English."

Marcel was speechless for a moment, but finally said, "What about Amanda?"

"What about her? We're free to see other people."

"Since when?"

Cricket laughed. "Since forever. It's nothing real serious. We like each other's company and the sex is good, but we're not thinking about moving in together or anything."

The sex is good, Marcel thought. *Jesus. I could've gone another forty-two years without hearing that.*

"She's really cute," Cricket said. "Or did I say that already?"

"Yes. You said that already."

"But I've got some reservations about getting involved with someone I work with. You know what happened with Irma that time. Christ, what a mistake *that* was."

"So is this one a lesbian at least?" Marcel queried with a tinge of sarcasm. She was upset by this entire conversation. How could Cricket be interested in someone else when she had Amanda?

"Yes, she's a lesbian. I verified that already." She laughed again. "Hey, I'm getting Spurs tickets tomorrow. The Lakers are in town. You interested in coming with us? Amanda's been talking about this new restaurant downtown. It'll be fun."

"I don't think so. Thanks."

"Why not? You never have time for your friends anymore!

Now that you're retired, you do even less than you used to do."

"Still not going."

"Well, if you won't go to the game, then at least have dinner with us at the new place, okay? Okay. I'm hanging up now and making the reservations. Sebastian's at River Center Mall. Be there at six."

Marcel was still peeved at Cricket for several reasons, but the one that weighed heaviest on her mind at the moment was the way Cricket had given her no choice but to have dinner with them Friday night. Marcel wasn't sure which was worse, seeing Amanda again or not seeing her again. This was a no-win situation, and she felt depressed about her options.

Once the three of them were together, however, Marcel felt a little better. It was easy keeping the conversation flowing with Cricket at the table. Cricket told them about a school dance that she had chaperoned and how keeping the kids in the gym and out of the oleanders had been her biggest problem.

"What about you?" Cricket asked Marcel finally. "How's the new business going?"

"We can't find a building we like. And we're both pretty tired of looking."

"And where are you interested in locating?" Amanda asked.

Marcel mumbled, "Yuppieville," and then went back to studying her menu. Her heart seemed to alternate between fluttering and sinking, depending on how Amanda looked at her or what she said. Marcel decided right then and there that she would never put herself in this position again. *Maybe it's time to tell Cricket how I feel about her girlfriend,* she thought with a sigh.

"Amanda's a Realtor," Cricket said. "Here you and Carmen have been scouring the city looking for a suitable place when Amanda can probably fix you right up!"

Marcel closed her eyes and slightly nodded. "That's a thought."

"Hey," Cricket said. "You've seen my house and you know what I paid for it. She's great!"

"Cricket, please," Amanda said. Her face was flushed with embarrassment. Marcel directed the conversation away from real estate and toward the Spurs and basketball in general. After dinner Marcel stood on the street corner and watched them walk toward the Alamodome with scores of other basketball fans, and more than anything in the world she wanted to be the one sitting next to Amanda that night.

Chapter Five

Marcel opened an eye and peeked at the clock on her nightstand. It was three-oh-one A.M. and everything was as perfect as she could get it. The temperature in the room was cool, but not too cool. The house was quiet except for an occasional popping or creaking that ordinarily accompanied an older home. The linen on the bed was just right — the sheets clean and crisp, the light blanket and bedspread folded back in a nice cuff resting on her shoulder. Marcel always went to bed nude for maximum comfort so that clothing didn't have a chance to spoil anything. The stage was set, and Marcel was its only player — there in bed, ready and waiting for the miracle of sleep to arrive.

Had she not yawned earlier while talking to her mother

on the phone, Marcel wouldn't have even considered going to bed yet, but all the signs had been there and she knew her body was beginning to surrender. Without making much of a fuss, she had hung up the phone, gone directly upstairs, taken off her clothes, and crawled between the covers. Now all she had to do was wait.

Glancing at the clock again, she noticed it was only three-oh-two A.M. If it didn't happen soon, then she feared it wouldn't happen at all tonight and she would have to get up and find something to do. The false alarms were frustrating, but Marcel knew better than to think about it. She stayed busy and slept when she could.

Stretching again and fluffing up her pillow for the fifth time, she settled back down and adjusted her covers. She closed her eyes once more, and the next time she opened them it was six-thirty A.M. She smiled and stretched again, feeling rested and refreshed. Her batteries had been sufficiently recharged.

It was still dark outside, but Marcel got up, took a shower, and dressed for the day. She was always conscious of what she liked to refer to as "bedroom psychology." She had trained herself to view her bed as serving only one purpose: It was the place where she slept. She never read there or watched television there. It was reserved for sleeping only. Period.

Marcel tried to keep her insomnia from taking over her life, and she had learned to look at it not so much as a dysfunction but as a uniqueness associated with her. Some people needed six to eight hours of sleep a night; Marcel could feel rested and refreshed after only two. That gave her twenty-two hours a day to do the things she liked to do, and in a way it all evened out.

She went downstairs and made a pot of decaf coffee. Her mother was in Denver playing in a high-stakes poker game and had similar gigs lined up in Kansas City, Reno, and Dallas over the next few days. Outside, Marcel found the newspaper in the driveway, and once she was back in the kitchen she located the classified ads and scanned the pages for any new commercial property that might be available for lease.

Marcel and Carmen had plans to meet later and discuss some new strategy. They both knew that it shouldn't take this long to find a suitable building. They were almost to the point of lowering their expectations. A few minutes later the telephone rang.

"Marcel?" the woman said. "This is Amanda. I hope I'm not calling too early."

Amanda, Marcel thought as her heart began to race. *Amanda!*

"Hi," Marcel managed to say, sounding much calmer than she felt. "Too early? Not at all. What can I do for you?"

"I wanted to apologize for last night and the way Cricket kept badgering you about using me as your Realtor."

"Badgering? I didn't —"

"She put you in an awkward position, and that wasn't fair to you," Amanda said.

Marcel could hear the intensity in her voice, and she wasn't sure where it was coming from.

"I don't know what's going on," Amanda continued, "but I've noticed a difference in you lately. You've been distant and sort of bored, frankly. If I've said or done something to offend you, then I wish you would tell me."

"Bored?" Marcel said, confused and surprised. *Bored?* she thought. *I'm crazy about you,* she wanted to say.

"I guess your reasons for disliking me don't matter," Amanda continued in a low, strained voice. "I just thought things were going well there for a while with the three of us."

"Amanda —"

"I can recommend several good Realtors for you if you're interested. Two are gay, if keeping it in the family is a priority. I'm sure they'll be able to help you find what you're looking for. This city is crawling with good commercial property for lease."

"Amanda, please."

"Please what?" she said, pronouncing the two words as if they were each long, drawn-out sentences.

Marcel nervously cleared her throat. "I'm sorry if I've seemed a bit spacey lately." She could feel the momentum building and that Robicheaux charm beginning to kick in. "With retirement and trying to get this new business off the ground, I've been distracted."

"Distracted is putting it mildly."

"I'm sorry."

"I know *distracted* when I see it, Marcel. I also know *bored* and *indifferent*. You haven't convinced me that there isn't a problem."

"Sounds like you're unwilling to be convinced."

"On the contrary."

Marcel noticed there was less stringency in Amanda's voice. "Getting this business started is proving more frustrating than anticipated. All I seem to do anymore is drive around and look at buildings that I don't like when all I really want to do is hang out at estate sales and repo warehouses and buy old furniture."

There was a pause before Amanda said, "Well, you've sure been in a pissy mood lately."

Marcel chuckled and slowly rubbed her eyes. "I'm sure I have, and I'm sorry."

"It's okay," Amanda said, the relief evident in her voice. "For some reason I thought it had something to do with me."

Marcel closed her eyes and sighed. She couldn't believe what was happening. "Sorry to disappoint you," she lied. *Oh, Jesus . . . was that flirting? Am I doing that again?* Marcel cleared her throat and gripped the phone tightly. "I was wondering if . . . uh . . . it looks like Carmen and I need a Realtor," she admitted lamely. "Can we meet with you sometime?"

~ ~ ~ ~ ~

50

Later that afternoon, Marcel and Carmen went to meet Amanda at an address Amanda had given them in Olmos Park. Just looking at the place from the outside, Marcel liked it right away.

"This is Yuppieville," Marcel said as she shielded her eyes and peered through the huge front window. "And it's got parking."

"No other antique shops or furniture stores in the area either," Carmen said as she looked up and down the street.

There was no indication that it was for lease other than the fact that the place was empty. It was on a busy corner with a four-way stop and in a nice, affluent older neighborhood.

Someone pulled up, and Marcel turned in time to see Amanda get out of her Lincoln Town Car. It was a company car, with Bradford Realty on the side, but impressive nonetheless. Amanda looked fabulous in a crème-colored dress and matching heels. Marcel forced herself to keep from staring at Amanda's legs. Immediately she knew that this whole arrangement wasn't a good idea, but she'd known that from the beginning and it hadn't stopped her.

"You found it," Amanda said. She had the keys to the building in one hand and a folder in the other. "Hi, Carmen."

"How long has this place been available?" Carmen asked.

Amanda got the door open, and the three of them went inside. "About a month now. The previous tenant died unexpectedly, and the building's owner lives out of state."

Carmen suddenly stopped in the middle of the huge room. "Where and how did the previous tenant die?" she asked.

Amanda held the folder close to her chest and studied Carmen for a moment, as if trying to determine why the question had been asked. "He died of a heart attack at his home."

Carmen turned slowly as she looked at the ceiling and the bare walls. "Do you feel it, Marcel?"

Marcel had been on alert the moment Carmen had asked her first question. Carmen was sensitive to certain types of spiritual energy, and this place had obviously set off some alarms for her somewhere.

"No," Marcel said, remembering a few times when she had experienced something similar just by being close to Carmen in such a situation.

Carmen cut her eyes over at her and said, "Your mind is somewhere else."

Marcel gave her a brief please-shut-up look while Amanda watched them, puzzled.

"Bad energy or good energy?" Marcel asked. Then with a smile she added, "Will we have to call a priest if we take it?"

"Good energy," Carmen said. "Female energy."

"*Very* good energy," Marcel said gleefully.

"What are you two talking about?" Amanda asked.

Carmen stopped turning and gave Amanda her complete attention. "So far this building has passed three of the four tests I have for it. There's parking, it's in Yuppieville, and it has good energy."

"I see," Amanda said. "What's the fourth?"

"Can we afford it?" Carmen said with a wink.

Amanda insisted on taking them to lunch, which turned out to be just as stressful as Marcel had anticipated. Amanda actually had two other places to show them, so they left Marcel's BMW there and let Amanda chauffeur them around in the Town Car.

"What kind of gas mileage do you get in this thing?" Carmen asked as she closed the door. Marcel had beaten her to the car and had already staked a claim on the backseat. She didn't want to be any closer to Amanda than was necessary.

"It's pitiful," Amanda said, "but I get a generous expense account, so I don't worry too much about it."

Marcel had chosen to sit behind Amanda so she saw only the back of her gorgeous blond head instead of her profile. Marcel made it a point to stare out the window and was grateful that Carmen kept the conversation going. A while later when everyone was quiet, Marcel looked up at the rearview mirror and saw Amanda staring back at her. Their eyes held for only a moment before Marcel glanced away. She didn't trust herself to look again, and she wondered how long Amanda had been staring at her and what she had been thinking.

At the restaurant, Carmen was her usual levelheaded self; she and Amanda worked out the details for leasing the building. They would sign the papers the next day and then Carmen and Marcel could begin renovations.

"When do you expect to be open for business?" Amanda asked.

"Three weeks at the latest," Carmen said. "I'll get my brothers in there, and you won't recognize the place."

Amanda asked Marcel, "Will you take consignments?"

"Yes," Marcel said. After a moment, she noticed them both looking at her expectantly. "As long as we have the space available," she added.

Amanda sighed heavily and directed the rest of her questions and the luncheon conversation to Carmen. All Marcel wanted to do was be someplace else — anyplace else as long as she was away from Amanda. She wasn't sure how much longer she could continue this charade. Marcel hated the fact that she might be in love with her.

On the way back to drop them off at Marcel's car, Amanda asked Carmen more specific questions about the business. "I think you two will do well," Amanda said as she parked beside Marcel's car.

They got out of the Town Car, and Carmen went over to peek in the store's window again. Amanda looked at Marcel with another puzzled expression.

"You've been very quiet," Amanda said.

"We've spent weeks looking for a place, and we like the first one you show us," Marcel said. "Thank you."

"Are you sure I haven't said or done something to make you uncomfortable?"

"Not at all," Marcel assured her, but she couldn't stand there and have this conversation. She pulled her keys from her pocket and started around the front of Amanda's car. "You'll let us know what time we can sign the paperwork tomorrow?"

"Yeah, sure," Amanda said as she opened her car door.

"Thanks again."

Amanda waved at Carmen from her car and stared at Marcel for a long time. With a push of a button, she rolled down the window on the passenger's side and leaned over in the seat and irritably said, "Marcel, I don't know what's going on with you, or what I've done to alienate you, but I find your distance and indifference very painful. I'm sorry we can't be friends." She pushed the button again and rolled the window back up, then pulled out of the parking lot and sped away, leaving Marcel standing there blinking.

Chapter Six

The following morning Marcel arrived at Carmen's house to pick her up for their appointment with Amanda. Carmen had insisted that Marcel get there early so that they could go over a few things about the business. Marcel pulled up her usual chair at Carmen's kitchen table, and without asking whether or not Marcel had eaten breakfast yet, Carmen whipped up potato-and-egg tacos and poured two tumblers of orange juice for them.

"I still can't get used to the idea that I'm not going to work in the mornings," Marcel said.

"Well, that's about to change."

"You know what I mean."

Carmen smiled. "Yes. I know what you mean. We'll both

have a new routine down before you know it. Remind me to call my brother after we leave Amanda's office. He'll meet us at the shop when we're finished there."

"Do you think we'll be able to get the place ready in three weeks?" Marcel asked. She smiled as she reached for a steaming tortilla, which looked remarkably like one of the Dakotas.

Carmen nodded. "Sure. As long as you get the utilities turned on soon. We can't work in the dark, you know."

"Hey," Marcel said with a wink. "I've done some of my best work in the dark."

Carmen smirked. "Not lately you haven't."

Marcel let that remark slide and then promised to take care of the utilities that afternoon. "When can I start buying furniture?"

Carmen laughed. "As soon as you get the books set up, the software for the inventory loaded, our sign ordered and installed, lines painted in the parking lot, the bank account opened, merchant card service online for credit cards, our offices furnished, the windows —"

Marcel shook her head and growled a little. "Forget it. Just give me a list."

Marcel wrote a check for two months' rent and signed the lease agreement. Amanda was reserved and cool, no doubt a direct result of Marcel's attempts to keep distance between them. *Okay,* Marcel thought. *Mission accomplished. I've pushed her away, and that's what I wanted.* Sliding the papers across Amanda's desk, she looked up into the bluest eyes she'd ever seen. *So why do I feel like throwing myself under a train?* Marcel wondered hopelessly.

"Do you have any questions about the lease?" Amanda asked. "Or the building?" She leaned over and gave Carmen two sets of keys. "If not, then I wish you both the best of luck in your new business. As soon as you're open, I plan to do some shopping there."

Amanda's pale blue seersucker jacket made her eyes look radiant, and her white silk blouse and dark blue skirt gave her a professional and serious demeanor that Marcel was drawn to.

"Are you looking for a particular piece of furniture?" Marcel asked. "Or will you just be shopping?"

"I'll be shopping."

Carmen stood up, and Marcel knew that she was ready to go now that they had the keys to the building. Marcel was in a hurry to leave as well and wasn't about to let her hormones get in the way again. Earlier, she'd only been gnawing on those ties to Amanda, but now it was time to sever them.

"Thanks for your help," Marcel said.

"I hope it wasn't too painful," Amanda replied.

Carmen shoved the keys in her pocket. "We've wasted nearly a month looking for the right building. And no telling how much gas." She slapped Marcel on the back. "But we got to know the city pretty well!"

Amanda opened her office door for them. "I'm glad I could help. It was nice seeing you again, Carmen."

"Likewise," Carmen said.

Marcel waited for Amanda to say something else to her — all the while *wanting* her to and then at the same time *not* wanting her to — but all Amanda did was continue to hold the door open and glare at her.

With hands shaking and her heart filling with sadness, Marcel said, "Thanks again for your help."

"My pleasure."

Marcel zipped out of the parking lot and sped through traffic as though she were driving the getaway car in a bank robbery, but she came to her senses as soon as she heard Carmen whistling the theme song to *Highway Patrol*.

"Don't you have to call your brother or something?" Marcel asked with a tinge of irritation.

Carmen rummaged through her backpack and found her cell phone. After she hung up with her brother, she drummed her fingers on the dash in a semblance of nonchalance. A few moments later Carmen said, "Out with it. Why are you treating Amanda like a third-class citizen? I thought you two got along okay."

"We do," Marcel said. "We get along fine."

"You said next to nothing at lunch yesterday and even less today. The tension between you two —"

"I can't talk about this right now," Marcel said quietly. "I'm sorry."

"Okay." Carmen glanced out the window. "It's not like I don't know already."

"Know what?"

"That you think you're in love with her."

"I can't talk about this right now."

Marcel gripped the steering wheel tightly and took a deep breath. *The hard part is over,* she thought. *Over and done. Now stop whining about it.*

Renovation work at the shop moved along steadily once they got started. Carmen and three of her brothers began transforming the front portion of the interior into a classy showroom. With Heidi Cooper's help over the weekend, they painted the ceiling and walls white and added track lighting to emphasize the two front windows where they'd have their best furniture pieces displayed. The woodwork along the baseboards and doorframes was being varnished, and Carmen was in the process of refinishing the counter.

Marcel's tasks seemed just as endless, but each little thing that she was able to check off her list became a major accomplishment. By the time Cricket arrived Friday afternoon with enough fried chicken and French fries to feed everyone, it was easy to see progress.

"This place is looking good," Cricket said, "but I hate that paint smell."

All work stopped as they followed Cricket and the fried chicken into what would eventually become Carmen's work area.

"Where's your mother?" Cricket asked Marcel as she set the box of chicken down on a workbench. "Don't tell me she's not here! You think I came just to see you?"

"She's in Honolulu," Marcel said with a laugh. "Won't be back until next week, which means you're stuck with us."

"But you can go now," Carmen said. "As long as you leave the chicken."

Their laughter echoed through the huge empty space, and Marcel had a good feeling about what they were doing and where they were doing it. *All that female energy,* she thought.

After their lunch break, Carmen and her crew went back to work on the showroom and left Marcel and Cricket to clean up the mess made from lunch.

"I have a favor to ask you," Cricket said after a moment. Her red hair had that fresh, windblown look, and her voice had taken on a low, conspiratorial tone.

"Sure. What's up?"

"I need a fourth for miniature golf tonight." Cricket picked up a wad of napkins and stray chicken bones and shoved them in the empty box. "Say you'll do it. Please?"

"I'm planning on being tired later," Marcel said. Hell, she was already exhausted and sore in a few places she forgot she had. She'd made a nice dent in her list of things to do today, and even though none of it was grunt work along the lines of what Carmen was doing, Marcel was still achy from bending, reaching, and cleaning the offices.

"I know my timing isn't the greatest," Cricket said, "but

I've got myself in a bit of a pickle. It's that new teacher I work with. I've invited her out for miniature golf . . . like on a date, sort of. Well, it's more like Amanda and I had plans for miniature golf and I invited Naomi to go with us, sort of." She shrugged innocently. "I . . . uh . . . sort of need for you to be her date."

Marcel laughed. "Sort of?"

"Yeah. Sort of."

"Not on your life."

"But you have to!"

"A blind date? Are you serious? Absolutely not."

"It's not like that exactly."

"It's not like *what* exactly?" Marcel said. "Sounds like a blind date to me. You and Amanda and me and some woman I've never met. What would you call it?"

"You met her at your retirement party, so don't give me that blind date excuse."

"I don't remember meeting anyone new at my party."

"It doesn't matter. Just do it. I need for you to be there," Cricket said. Her voice suddenly had a familiar edge to it, and Marcel realized that Cricket was close to tears.

"Hey. What's the matter with you?"

"I said please, already," Cricket reminded her with a sniff. "This is important to me. I want —"

"Okay, okay," Marcel said, puzzled about Cricket's intensity. "What's up with you all of a sudden?"

"I said it was important. Why do you need to know more than that?"

Marcel nodded. "You're right. But don't expect me to be very good company. I worked hard today."

Cricket sniffed again. "Then you'll do it?"

"Do I have a choice?"

"Oh, thank you, thank you, thank you!" Cricket threw her arms around her and hugged her fiercely. She was so grateful that Marcel started to feel guilty for ever having said no in the first place.

~ ~ ~ ~ ~

Marcel was tired, but not sleepy, and as she got out of the shower and thought about what she was going to wear that night, she tried very hard not to be miffed at Cricket. *I'm forty-two years old and going on a date with a woman I can't remember meeting. What the hell was I thinking? How did I let her talk me into this?* And not only was there the blind date thing to worry about, but now Marcel had to spend more time with Amanda. It had been a week since she and Carmen had signed the papers in Amanda's office, and Marcel wasn't sure if she was up to that again so soon.

She remembered the directions Cricket had given her, but more or less found Golf World by accident. Marcel was the first to arrive and ended up talking to four German tourists who were waiting their turn to tee off. She enjoyed practicing her German on them and talked briefly about places in Germany which they were all familiar with. Twenty minutes later, Cricket and Amanda strolled up with a short, petite woman beside them. The woman had met them on the sidewalk after having come from a different part of the parking lot.

"Marcel!" Cricket said. "This is Naomi Shapiro. A friend from school."

"We met at your retirement party the other night," Naomi said to Marcel. "But you were a bit overwhelmed at the time."

Marcel couldn't remember ever seeing her before, and Marcel noticed right away that Amanda was both surprised by, as well as uncomfortable with, the sudden change of events. Marcel also recognized the sexual energy in the air and the animation in Cricket's eyes and voice as she yakked away. Cricket's gushing over this woman was obvious, and Amanda and Marcel briefly traded questioning looks . . . and once again Marcel was forced to admit what a stunningly beautiful woman Amanda was. Dressed in white shorts, a pale yellow shirt neatly tucked in, and new white sneakers and ankle-high socks, Amanda was definitely "babe" material, as Cricket would say. The yellow shirt brought out the blondness of her shoulder-length hair, and just seeing her again made Marcel's pulse quicken.

Marcel took a deep breath and decided to focus her attention on her miniature golf game instead of being pissed at Cricket.

They selected clubs, chose golf balls in their favorite colors, and decided what order they'd play in. Marcel was up first and aced the hole, which gave her a chance to stand back and watch the others play. After two minutes of giggling and whispering between Cricket and Naomi, a light finally went on in Marcel's head. She wasn't there as Naomi's "date." She was there to make Cricket and Naomi's *first* date look less blatant. *Focus on your game and not being mad at Cricket,* she reminded herself.

On the second hole, Marcel made another hole-in-one and let them boo her into a better mood. She had always been good at this game, and she realized that she might accidentally have fun despite the irritating behavior Cricket was displaying. Cricket and Naomi were like two teenagers on a sugar high, and as far as Marcel could tell, Amanda seemed to be handling it remarkably well. Had Cricket been Marcel's lover, however, Marcel would've already left fifteen minutes ago.

When Amanda's turn approached, Marcel watched with acute interest as Amanda sank a putt for par and reached down to retrieve her blue golf ball from the cup. Amanda's legs were once again Marcel's main focus, and they again reminded her of a grace that bordered on perfection. Marcel couldn't imagine having this woman as a lover and then openly flirting with someone else the way Cricket was doing. Amanda was the type of woman who could change your whole life with just a smile. *Listen to me,* Marcel thought. *Thinking like a sappy romantic again.*

The only evidence of Amanda's irritation with Cricket's

behavior was the way she held her golf club and began tap-tap-tapping it against the green carpeted surface of the tiny fake golf course. What was even more amazing to Marcel was the way Cricket either didn't notice or didn't care how her actions were affecting others. Cricket was in fine form as she turned up the charm another notch. Marcel had seen this side of her many times over the years when Cricket was on the trail of a woman whom she found attractive.

"What a great haircut, Naomi," Cricket said. "Who does it for you?" She reached over and touched Naomi's hair, which made Amanda's golf club begin tapping much harder.

"Cricket," Marcel said. "It's your turn."

"Oh! So it is."

As Cricket stepped up to her yellow ball, Marcel leaned over and whispered, "If you don't stop flirting with her, I swear I'm gonna kick your butt all the way back to the car."

Cricket's golf ball zoomed across the sixth and seventh hole and landed in a fishpond beside the German foursome.

"Look what you did!" Cricket screeched. She whirled around to see who else had noticed her wayward shot, while the Germans up ahead were looking back to see where the ball had come from.

In shock, Amanda said, "Cricket, what are you doing?"

"It was Marcel's fault!"

The nice German man had fished the ball out of the pond and was on his way toward them. Horrified, Cricket hid her face behind her hands while Amanda, Naomi, and Marcel laughed heartily. Marcel thanked him in German and apologized for her friend with the bad form and manners. When he left she gave the ball back to Cricket and said, "We'll pretend that one never happened."

"What did he say?" Cricket asked meekly, still shaking from the experience.

"He was letting us know that you killed a fish over there. A direct hit to the head. Now pay attention to what you're doing."

As Cricket lined up her putter with the ball again, Amanda maneuvered closer to Marcel. "You speak German," she said. "And very well, from what I heard."

"I do okay."

"What other languages do you speak?"

"I'm fluent in French," Marcel said, "but with a name like Robicheaux, I guess I should be. And enough Korean to keep me out of trouble." From the corner of her eye, she caught Cricket touching Naomi's hair again. "Cricket," Marcel said. "Much better shot." She drilled her with a keep-your-hands-to-yourself look, and Cricket immediately obeyed.

After the game was over, they had coffee at Java Joe's. Amanda and Cricket sat on one side of the booth while Naomi and Marcel were on the other. Amanda was across from Marcel, which made it hard for Marcel to concentrate on anything else. Naomi, however, seemed to suddenly discover that Marcel was there. She fired off several questions and commented on how young Marcel looked to have already retired. She then asked about Marcel's Army career and where she'd been stationed.

"You're not exactly what I was expecting," Naomi said.

"Were you picturing combat boots and hand grenades?" Cricket asked. Everyone at the table laughed, and Marcel took Cricket's teasing in stride.

"She cleans up pretty good though," Cricket said. "I have to admit that."

"Was that a compliment?" Marcel asked sweetly.

Cricket smirked and volunteered to get them all coffee refills. She insisted that Naomi go with her to help carry them. Marcel made a mental note to have a little talk with her later. Cricket had a tendency to get herself into trouble without even knowing it.

"What did you say to her earlier?" Amanda asked,

interrupting Marcel's thoughts. "Just before Cricket sent that golf ball into Oklahoma territory."

Marcel laughed. "I don't even remember."

"I see," Amanda said. "You don't like questions, do you?"

"Hmm. What makes you say that?" Marcel suddenly wished that Cricket and Naomi would hurry back. "I don't mind questions at all."

"Or is it questions from me that you don't like?"

"Where did you get that idea?"

"I asked you a question and you pretended not to remember."

"Pretended?"

Amanda leaned back in the booth. "Never mind. It doesn't matter."

"Amanda, I —"

"How is the work on the building coming?" Amanda asked impatiently.

Marcel was surprised and flustered at Amanda's irritation. It had appeared suddenly, and Marcel wasn't quite sure what to do about it.

"Work on the building?" Amanda said. "Or is that another question you're choosing not to answer?"

Marcel blinked several times and then shook her head. "Carmen has the renovations under control," she said lamely. "Drapes and carpeting are going in tomorrow. It's shaping up."

"When will you be open for business?"

"In about a week, hopefully."

"That's very ambitious," Amanda said.

Still a bit uncomfortable with Amanda's stiff, formal tone, Marcel said, "They've worked hard. And it looks good. You wouldn't recognize the place."

"Maybe I'll drop by some afternoon next week and check it out." After a moment, Amanda seemed to relax a little. "I like this much better," she said quietly. "I like the Marcel who has time for her friends and isn't quite so preoccupied." She smiled weakly, and Marcel could feel her heart melting in her chest. "I've missed you," Amanda said. "Whatever's bothering you I wish I could fix it."

You can, Marcel wanted to say. *You're the only one who can.*

Emotional honesty was still too new for her since keeping her feelings under wraps had become second nature. Four years at West Point and then twenty years in the Army — an eternity of either being a subordinate or having subordinates. Either way, it had done little to prepare Marcel for a life outside the military.

She had worked in a man's world for over half of her life and had done her job as well as, if not better than, her male counterparts. Marcel had been yelled at and disciplined by the best during her lengthy career, and she had done her share of yelling in return. Marcel's skin was thick, and she had learned to depend on her instincts. But Amanda Farley could unravel her down to the very core with no more than a look, a phrase, or the mere tilt of her blond head. Those three simple words, *I've missed you*, had Marcel in a state of paralysis — both emotionally and physically.

"And then there's the silence," Amanda said as her anger and confusion began to return. "A cool indifference that comes over you so quickly sometimes. It's new, and it frightens me." She stretched her arm across the back of the booth. "I keep wondering if it's something I've said or done. Or if there's something about me that irritates you. But then I keep reminding myself that everything can't always be about me." She put her elbows on the table and leaned forward. "So out with it, Marcel. Tell me why you're pulling away." Her voice shook with emotion.

Marcel felt like a rabbit that had accidentally hopped into an occupied wolf's den. There was no way out, and she felt totally powerless. Luckily for her, Cricket and Naomi returned to the table with their coffee. Marcel knew that she couldn't let things continue the way they were. She was going to have to talk to Cricket about this soon.

Chapter Seven

The grand opening of the Antique Villa came much more quickly than Marcel and Carmen had anticipated. At one point, three weeks had sounded like plenty of time, but the night before the opening they were still hanging drapes and working feverishly on selecting which furniture pieces would go where in order to best accent the huge display windows in the front. Each piece needed to be in its most flattering light, and they finally decided to let Roslin arrange everything.

"Decorating isn't the area of my expertise," Marcel said. "Where's a gay boy when you need one?"

The store was a classy place from almost every angle, beginning with the curb at the busy street where they were located and all the way to the utility closet where the brooms were kept. The parking lot had freshly painted stripes with handicapped spaces appropriately designated. Pansies of every imaginable color lined the sidewalk, and ornate planters showcased daisies with ivy spilling over the sides.

One of Marcel's responsibilities had been to get a sign for the storefront, and she had spent a good deal of time and money finding one that would preserve the flavor of the building and the neighborhood and still be unique so that it would draw a potential customer's attention. The sign painter whom Marcel had chosen had done an excellent job, using readable calligraphy against a tan-and-orange background. The sign had a definite European flavor to it and was not only the building's best feature, but it also added character to the entire block.

Much to Marcel's relief, the caterer was early for the opening. The bartender who accompanied them became busy almost immediately, thanks to Carmen and her brothers. The caterer was a friend of Carmen's and consisted of three gay siblings in their early thirties. The two sisters handled the food preparation while their brother was in charge of the blender, swizzle sticks, and all libations. Marcel noticed the strong family resemblance between them and liked the way they worked together. Roslin stepped in right away and took over the details about where and how the food would be set up. Thirty minutes before the guests were due to arrive, part of the showroom had been turned into a nice reception area with that savory meatball-swimming-in-mushroom-sauce aroma, which was causing stomachs to grumble right away. Carmen admitted to being more fond of the constant swoosh of the margarita machine as its contents tumbled into a frozen mixture behind the portable bar.

"It's like music to my ears," Carmen said, leaning closer to the machine and sighing heavily.

As the new owners, Marcel and Carmen met each guest at

the door and welcomed them. Antique Villa tours were given and little SOLD tags were gradually beginning to appear on many of the furniture pieces displayed.

Marcel noticed that Cricket, Amanda, Cricket's new friend, Naomi, and a few others had her mother surrounded and were in deep conversation near the mahogany armoire in the corner. Several people had arrived at the same time with Cricket and Amanda, so there had been little opportunity for chitchat with them. Amanda seemed more distant than Marcel could ever remember her being. In one way it was a relief, but in another way it saddened her. Marcel always felt so off balance whenever she was around Amanda, but keeping her emotions under control was becoming easier.

Marcel was surprised to see so many of her old coworkers there, and she gave them all extra-long hugs. It wasn't until she saw them again that she realized just how much she missed them. William, her former secretary, had quickly taken over the tour-guide duties, while Captain Heidi Cooper volunteered to be the official door-greeter. Out of uniform, she looked even younger, and her easygoing manner made her perfect for meeting guests as they came in. Heidi had been a frequent visitor to the shop in the afternoons and on weekends during the renovation process, and she had helped with a lot of the painting and varnishing. It was evident that she felt comfortable at the shop and knew her way around.

Family members, most of them Carmen's, were everywhere. Friends, acquaintances, old office mates, and members of the local chamber of commerce, as well as curiosity seekers from the neighborhood, were all there. The invitations sent and the flyers posted had produced a lively crowd. Some were dressed in formal attire, while others wore jeans and sneakers. Marcel and Carmen dressed up for the occasion, with Carmen in a black tux, looking remarkably like the bartender, and Marcel wearing a long gray dress embroidered with tiny flowers at the neckline with a matching chenille jacket. Several friends teased them about being such a cute couple. Carmen was what Marcel liked referring to as a handsome woman. Carmen had that perfect posture that came from years in the military, and she managed to keep fit by running every morning. She was taller than Marcel — in the five-ten range — and had thick, black hair that came just below her collar in the trendy little-boy style. With the opening of their new business being something they had talked about and planned on for years, they were now psyched and ready for this.

Marcel was conscious of the dinging of the door each time someone came in, as though her head had a string attached to the doorknob. She was dumbfounded when she looked up to see General Wheatly and his wife, Jordan, arrive, since she had purposely left them off the invitation list.

"General," Marcel said as she shook General Wheatly's hand. "What a surprise to see you!"

"Wouldn't miss it, Marcel. Retirement seems to have agreed with you."

"And Jordan," Marcel said. Jordan took her extended hand and then pulled her closer to kiss her cheek.

"You look great, darling," Jordan whispered breathily. Marcel wondered if Jordan watched old Mae West movies in her spare time. "I never miss an opportunity to see you again."

Marcel removed her hand and asked if she could get them something to drink. It didn't take long for others to notice that the General and his lovely wife had arrived. Marcel introduced Carmen as her business partner and was relieved when a few military people began to mingle in their direction. This was a rare opportunity for them to socialize with the boss, and Marcel was more than willing to accommodate them.

She stayed busy tending to other guests by answering questions about furniture pieces and the renovations on the building. A while later after the crowd had thinned out, Marcel found herself next to Cricket in the margarita line. It had been blatantly obvious all evening that Cricket's infatuation with Naomi was still an ongoing thing.

"What have you been up to lately?" Marcel asked. Cricket grinned and sipped her margarita. "You've been bad, haven't you?"

"But I'm so good when I'm bad."

"I'd hate to see you screw up something that's more important to you than you realize," Marcel said seriously.

"If you're referring to Amanda, then stop worrying. I'm just having a little fun." She stuck a fresh straw in her drink and frowned. "If Naomi would stop asking me questions about you I'd have a lot *more* fun, but I'm working on that."

"Questions about me?" Marcel said, surprised. She searched the crowd and saw Amanda talking to Jordan and Captain Cooper to the left of them, then found Naomi looking right at her across the room. Naomi smiled shyly and looked away again, but only seconds later Marcel saw her looking back to see if Marcel was still watching her.

"So," Cricket said. "I keep telling her that you aren't her type."

"And how do you know what her type is?"

"Because I'm her type, and you and I are nothing alike."

Marcel rolled her eyes. "I can't believe you're doing this," she said as she tried to keep her anger in check.

"Doing what? I'm having fun. Amanda doesn't own me. Jesus, Marcel. I pity the poor schmuck who finally gets stuck with you. It's that attached-at-the-hip attitude of yours that turns women off." Cricket laughed and poked her in the arm. "And speaking of attached at the hip, did you hear about the Siamese twins who moved to England so the other one could drive?"

Carmen had her bow tie undone and the top two buttons on her ruffled shirt open as she helped Marcel with the cleanup. Marcel was tired and knew instinctively that she would have no trouble sleeping later. She glanced at the grandfather clock across the showroom and was pleased to see that it was well after midnight already.

"One of the caterers was asking about you," Carmen said.

Marcel was caught off guard by the comment, but she didn't take it too seriously. "With my luck it was the brother."

"There you go again," Carmen said, shaking her head. "As a matter of fact, it was the cute tall one. Damn it, Marcel. Any woman who could keep me in edible finger food would have my undivided attention. What's the matter with you? It's like you're walking around in a fog these days."

"You said she asked about me," Marcel reminded her in an effort to change the subject. "What did she want to know?"

"She asked if you were single or if you had been in any twelve-step programs. Drinking habits. Were you dating. Ever married. You know. The usual."

Marcel smiled as she threw away a plastic cup with cigarette butts in it. Since there had been no smoking allowed inside, she had no idea where they had come from.

"Just tell her I still live with my mother and that should take care of any other questions she has."

"It probably would if you had an ordinary mother." Carmen stretched until her bones popped. "But your mother's ten times cooler than you are."

Marcel laughed and knew it was true.

"I made some interesting observations tonight," Carmen said as she gracefully hopped up on the counter. "And I have a few questions to ask you."

"And your observations were?" Marcel asked. These types of conversations were just one of the many reasons that Marcel treasured this woman's friendship. Carmen would tell her things she needed to know but didn't necessarily want to hear. In many ways they were still growing as friends, and each time there was an intense exchange between them, Marcel was usually left with a new realization about herself.

These sessions weren't always a pleasant experience, but the results were usually rewarding.

"Three women were watching you tonight," Carmen said. "I talked to all three of them at some point, and got some very interesting answers."

"How many of those margaritas did you have?" Marcel asked skeptically.

"First, there was the caterer," Carmen said, ignoring her. "I've already told you what we discussed. She did say that you were hot and that she could really learn to like antiques."

"Antiques? Hmm. Was she talking about me or the furniture?"

Carmen grinned. "The furniture. Then there was Jordan Wheatly. How did you ever get mixed up with that one, anyway?"

Marcel sighed and let out a frustrated groan.

"She was very interested in who you were seeing and how you were spending your time. She didn't sound or act like a woman who would settle for a kiss and a love pat. There was definitely lust in her eyes when she looked at you."

"Oh please," Marcel said. "She wants a fling. I'm sorry, but that's not me." She leaned against the counter beside Carmen's swinging, tuxedoed legs. "And I'm sure if you had watched her long enough, you could've seen that lusty look no matter which woman she was zeroing in on."

Carmen laughed. "That's true. She has an interest in Heidi Cooper, and she spent some time talking with Amanda. It's hard to say what Jordan's up to."

"Amanda," Marcel said with a sigh. She was more than ready to talk about something else now.

"Yes, Amanda," Carmen said. "She's so upset with you that she wouldn't even discuss it."

Marcel could feel her body begin to tingle just hearing Amanda's name. "How do you know she was upset?"

"Just a feeling." Carmen shrugged. "Nothing more. But,"

she said, "there was someone else I got some serious vibes from. She's a friend of Cricket's. I remember her from your retirement party."

Naomi, Marcel thought with a chuckle. *Cricket's new infatuation.*

"When she watched you it was with a different intensity than the other two."

"Different how?" Marcel asked. Carmen had her attention now. The first few times they'd had this kind of discussion, Marcel had been a nonbeliever in Carmen's uncanny ability to read people and "know" things, but not anymore. Carmen had been right too many times to not give credence to her insight. Marcel was a believer, and she listened carefully now to what Carmen had to say.

"The other two would like to . . . uh . . . bed you," Carmen said diplomatically. "But this one wants to know you." The soft thud of Carmen's black suede boots against the side of the counter gradually stopped.

"What about Cricket?" Marcel asked.

When Carmen didn't answer, Marcel said, "Cricket is interested in her."

Carmen nodded. "An unusual little foursome." Her boots began lightly thumping against the counter again. "How serious are you about Amanda?"

Marcel closed her eyes and took a deep breath. "I don't know."

"Have you thought about talking to Amanda about it?"

"Of course not," Marcel said with a tinge of panic in her voice.

"So you plan on doing nothing?"

"I'm open for suggestions."

"Amanda deserves to know why you're being so weird. And if you can't tell her, then maybe you should stop *being* weird. Have you tried that?"

"I've tried everything," Marcel said. "I've tried ignoring

my feelings. I've tried ignoring Cricket and Amanda." She looked up at Carmen and gave her a tired smile. "I've even tried not being so weird. Nothing works."

"Then stay busy and find other things to do," Carmen suggested. "Maybe it's time you went on a statewide buying spree. Take the truck on the road and hit some estate sales in Dallas and Houston. Don't come back until the truck's full." Carmen jumped down from the counter. "Or think about taking your mother with you. She likes spending money almost as much as you do."

"I'll consider it."

Chapter Eight

Marcel and Cricket were meeting for dinner at Chili's in the Quarry, and it was still amazing to Marcel how land developers could turn a huge hole in the ground into a shopper's paradise. As she pulled into the crowded parking lot, she noticed that Cricket's car was already there, but Marcel got a shock when she went inside and found not only Cricket, but also Amanda and Naomi waiting for her as well. Marcel had planned to tell Cricket about her feelings for Amanda over dinner. Now it was apparent that she should have been more specific about their meeting being for only the two of them.

"There you are!" Cricket said, and then turned her attention to the person in charge of seating them.

Marcel was fuming and couldn't believe that her

discussion with Cricket would again have to be delayed. Having tiptoed around this whole thing long enough, Marcel decided right then that somehow she would have a talk with Cricket later that evening.

They were shown to a table and even before their drink orders were taken, Naomi began asking her questions about antiques and inquiring about the business. After only a few minutes, Marcel felt herself relaxing as she talked about china cabinets and different kinds of wood. They were well into the entrée phase of dinner before she noticed that Cricket was annoyed at Naomi's interest. Marcel, however, was still upset with Cricket for not telling her that the other two would be joining them, so she didn't waste much time feeling bad about anything.

"How did you first get interested in antiques?" Naomi asked.

Marcel had never thought much about it before, but reasoned that all her life she'd been surrounded by old furniture, paintings, and jewelry. Such things gave her comfort in a strange way, and she had no other explanation for it.

Marcel said, "In my mother's line of work, she's had rare and unusual furniture pieces in our home ever since I could remember. Some stayed longer than others, but I've always loved them."

Cricket and Amanda chuckled.

"I met your mother the other night at the grand opening," Naomi said. "What a delightfully unusual woman."

"Can you spell *babe*?" Cricket said under her breath.

Eyes wide with surprise, Naomi asked Marcel if her mother was a lesbian, which made them all laugh heartily.

"Only in my dreams," Cricket said.

After dinner, Cricket announced that she had four movie passes to a romantic comedy that would begin in forty-five minutes.

"Where'd you get movie passes?" Amanda asked, her tone a shade above indifferent. She had been very quiet all evening.

"Radio trivia contest on the way home from work," Cricket said. "I knew the name of the Little Rascals' dog, and when I went to pick up the tickets this afternoon I begged for two more." She smiled impishly at Marcel before saying, "And they're only good for tonight, so everybody has to go."

"I see," Marcel said, and just as she was about to give her regrets, Naomi asked her another question and distracted her. They talked about women at West Point and being gay in the military. And as the four of them left the restaurant and ambled down the sidewalk toward the theater, Marcel got so caught up in explaining the absurd complexities of don't-ask-don't-tell that they were already inching toward the theater lobby before she realized what had happened.

Damn, Marcel thought as she took the ticket that was being handed to her. *Looks like I'm going to the movies.*

Once they were inside the theater, Cricket orchestrated the seating arrangements and wanted to be between Amanda and Naomi. Cricket then suggested to Marcel that she sit on the other side of Naomi. On the surface this all seemed quite innocent, until the lights went down and the feature started. In the dark, Marcel noticed right away how Cricket's hand covered Naomi's on the armrest. She felt herself getting angry at Cricket's boldness. *If I can see it,* Marcel thought, *then Amanda can see it. I've gotta have a talk with her.*

During the movie, Marcel had found it hard to concentrate, but she had been relieved about not having to sit close to Amanda in the theater. That would've been unbearable — the intimacy of darkness, the faint smell of Amanda's perfume, the knowledge of her closeness, the knowledge that she was there and yet unavailable, untouchable, and, even worse, uninterested. *The three U's,* Marcel thought as she pursed her lips. *Add un-fucking-fair to that while you're at it.*

Marcel was relieved when the movie was finally over and the lights came up. She wanted to go home and finish putting together the ad that she planned to run in the paper next week. Each time she had started working on it, she'd gotten sleepy, and with any luck at all tonight the same thing would happen.

"I need to talk to you tomorrow," Marcel whispered to Cricket as they let themselves be carried along in the clutch of people in the crowded aisle.

"About what?"

The thought of Cricket being so obvious in her pursuit of Naomi right under Amanda's nose infuriated her.

"Naomi!" Marcel snapped in her ear.

"I can tell you like her too! Don't get any ideas. I'm working on something."

"I'm not interested in her, you moron," Marcel hissed in Cricket's ear. "And you shouldn't be either!"

"Who are you? My mother?"

"Come by the shop tomorrow afternoon," Marcel said. Then, as she remembered the entourage that had shown up for dinner with them tonight, she added, "Alone."

Once they were outside the theater, Marcel noticed how peeved Amanda was. It reminded her of the day Amanda had taken Carmen and her to lunch. There was that same intensity in her eyes and tightness around the mouth that signaled acute displeasure. Marcel easily concluded that Amanda had seen Cricket's hand on Naomi's during the movie. Marcel thought, *After Amanda yells at her sufficiently later, I'll do more of it tomorrow.*

As they headed back to Chili's where their cars were parked, Cricket seemed to be attempting to coax Amanda into a better mood. They reached Marcel's car first and broke into polite good-byes and promises to do it again soon.

Marcel took the long way home and mulled over what she would say to Cricket the next day. Being a firm believer in the truth, she just wanted this over with so that maybe these little surprise get-togethers would stop happening.

Marcel pulled into her huge, winding driveway and set the motion light near the garage into action. Her mother was in Canada for a few days and had plans to play in another high-stakes game in Hong Kong several days after that. Depending on how Roslin did in those two places would determine where she would be over the next few months. Marcel liked the arrangement they had. Her mother was usually gone long enough for Marcel to miss her, and they were never at home together long enough to get in each other's way.

Marcel turned on several lights in the house and selected a Janis Ian CD to work by. She sorted through various graphics for the ad that she was putting together, and before she got too far into it, the doorbell rang. Marcel looked at her watch. It was already after eleven. At the door, she cautiously asked who was there.

"It's Amanda. I need to talk to you."

Marcel fumbled with the lock and swung the huge door open. "Come in," she said. "Where's Cricket?"

"She's at that new club that just opened. Apparently she knows the two women who own it."

With her heart thumping, Marcel led the way to the living room and turned the music down. "Have a seat," she said, indicating one of two sofas in the room. "Would you like something to drink?"

"No thanks," Amanda said. "I'm sorry I didn't call first."

"I'm usually up no matter what time it is." She could tell

that Amanda was upset, and a sense of dread was creeping through Marcel's body. *What if she's guessed how I feel? What if she's here to tell me to get a life, for crissakes?*

Marcel nervously cleared her throat. "Please sit down. The sofa's much more comfortable than it looks."

Amanda shook her head, walked over to the stereo, and picked up the empty CD case. "I don't understand what's happening to me," she said. "Not at all. When the three of us are together, I'm fine. We have fun, and I look forward to seeing you." Amanda stopped and turned around. Her blond hair was always perfect, and her blue eyes had the ability to melt Marcel right where she stood. "But then something happened and you wouldn't tell me about it," she said. "I know you've been staying away from us on purpose, and it's eating me up inside."

Amanda raised her hand to stop Marcel from speaking. "Please let me finish," she said. "I have a lot to say before I go. Most of it is coming in spurts, so I know I'm not making much sense. And some of it is about that obnoxious *Naomi* woman!"

Ah, Marcel thought as a light went on in her head. *Here we go. So she did see Cricket holding Naomi's hand earlier.* Marcel sighed and recalled that this wasn't the first time that she had been a sounding board for one of Cricket's lovers. She was used to the role and felt comfortable with it.

"What about that Naomi woman?" Marcel asked tiredly as she sat on the arm of the sofa.

Amanda started pacing, and she clenched her hands as she spoke. "Cricket is infatuated with her right now. The touchy-feely thing and the calls late at night. I've seen it. I'm not blind. And none of this is even new to me. She goes through things like this all the time," she said matter-of-factly. "Being Cricket's lover takes a lot of patience." Amanda glanced over at Marcel and threw her hands up in the air. "You've known her longer than anyone. I don't have to tell you how it is."

"I'm sure there's nothing serious between them, if that's what you're thinking," Marcel said.

"That's the least of my worries right now," Amanda assured her with a wave of her hand. She started pacing again and seemed to be collecting her thoughts, then suddenly said, "It's *you* that's making me crazy! I find myself being more concerned about Naomi sitting beside you when we're out somewhere. It makes me instantly angry. Or I go nuts when she has your complete attention while she's asking you those endlessly mundane questions. And I *hated* the thought of her being your date tonight."

Ding, ding, ding went that little bell in Marcel's head. *Amanda has been thinking about me . . .*

Confused, Marcel said, "She wasn't my date. I didn't even know you and Naomi were going to be there."

"Like that matters," Amanda grumbled. "The first time it happened was the night we played miniature golf," she continued. "Even though Cricket was attempting to flirt with her, it was no secret that Naomi was there as your date. That made me so jealous that I couldn't think about anything else. I was furious. Then we went to that coffee bar, and Naomi was sitting beside you." She lowered her voice and visibly forced herself to calm down. "I wanted to be the one sitting beside you. Me. Not her."

Marcel was too stunned to move. All she could see was blond hair and blue eyes coming toward her.

"And then tonight at the movie," Amanda said, her voice still low as she moved closer. "Cricket tried holding Naomi's hand in the beginning, and still all I could think about was you . . . you being two people away from me. Your sitting next to Naomi. Her hearing your laughter . . . maybe even feeling the heat of your body."

Amanda was close enough to her now that Marcel was indeed aware of Amanda's perfume. Their eyes locked, and the pounding of Marcel's heart obliterated the music filtering from the stereo.

"You," Amanda whispered. "It's always you now. Every thought. Every ache. Oh god, Marcel. If I don't kiss you I'll —"

The rest of Amanda's sentence was lost as she kissed Marcel in a wave of passion. Marcel went into immediate sensory overload. She was in Amanda's arms and could feel Amanda's breasts pressing against her. The kiss deepened as neither held anything back, and they both wanted more, more, more.

Marcel felt as though she were free-falling in a sea of warm, nurturing liquid as Amanda held her tight. Their breathing was ragged when they pulled away from each other, but within seconds they were kissing deeply again.

Amanda's hand covered Marcel's left breast and found a hard nipple begging for attention. "I have to touch you," Amanda said in a raspy voice as she slipped her hands under Marcel's shirt. "All of you."

Without another thought, Marcel got them on the sofa where the kissing began all over again and Marcel's hands were just as busy as Amanda's were. The intensity of Amanda's desire delighted Marcel. Amanda was wild and hungry, her lips moving from the cool flesh of Marcel's throat and bare shoulder to her cheek and then back again to Marcel's eager mouth.

"Is your mother home?" Amanda whispered in a voice laced with urgency.

"No," Marcel said as the warmth continued rushing through her. "She's in Montreal."

Their kiss instantly deepened before Amanda began shedding her clothes in earnest. Marcel tried not to let the impact of their actions cloud her thoughts, and she pushed the words *This is Cricket's lover* from her conscience.

"You've wanted this, too," Amanda said breathlessly while kissing Marcel's throat.

Marcel trembled as Amanda's hands roamed over her bare back.

"How long?" Amanda asked in a whisper. "Touch me," Amanda ordered. "Oh god, Marcel. Please touch me."

Amanda's long, tanned legs were open and inviting, and her hips rose to meet Marcel's hand. Marcel sighed as she began a gentle stroking. She took a swollen nipple into her mouth and set Amanda off on a wild, bucking ride to pleasure. Amanda wound her fingers through the back of Marcel's hair and heatedly urged her to take more of her breast into her mouth.

"Oh god yes. Like that. Like that!"

Amanda's climax would have thrown them both off the sofa had it not been for their pretzelike embrace. Amanda's entire body trembled and shook from orgasm, and Marcel felt a much needed warm release of her own finally take over.

Marcel kissed Amanda's nipple before releasing it completely, but kept her fingers in place inside of her. She gently kissed her cheek.

"I knew it," Amanda whispered groggily. "I knew it would be like this with you."

"Like what?" Marcel whispered. She was still overwhelmed by Amanda's being there and their urgent lovemaking. Marcel continued kissing Amanda's throat and chin, her fingers still inside Amanda and beginning to move slowly. Marcel was consumed with delight and emotion as Amanda once more responded to her. The hips were reaching for her, and it was apparent that Amanda was unafraid of demanding more. Marcel was there to take her over the edge again as many times as Amanda would let her. That would never be a problem.

"Like what?" Marcel whispered again while her fingers continued dancing between Amanda's legs.

"Like this," Amanda said in a harsh, raspy voice, and then

she started thrashing wildly on the sofa as she came. "Like this! God yes! Like this. Like this!"

Marcel held her until Amanda's breathing returned to normal and her body relaxed. Her fingers remained in place just in case she got another opportunity to please her again.

"Does this mansion have any bedrooms?" Amanda asked a few minutes later.

Marcel smiled and kissed her lightly on the lips. "Five, as a matter of fact. Which one would you like to see?"

"It doesn't matter. I want to make love to you in a bed." She put her arms around Marcel and kissed her deeply. "A big bed. Right now."

Chapter Nine

Marcel led the way to her bedroom without any thought to her "psychology" that it be used solely as a sleeping chamber. Her room happened to be the closest room at the top of the stairs.

She switched on the lamp beside the huge antique sleigh bed and noticed immediately how inviting the room appeared. Marcel imagined it looking like the master bedroom in a classy brothel, just by the way the bed was the room's main focus. If the house were a paragraph and Marcel's room were a sentence, then the bed would have been the only word on the entire page to have been set off in bold print.

Marcel turned from the lamp and saw Amanda's flawless body in the soft, sensual light. Even the way she moved made Marcel's heart skip a beat as Amanda came toward her.

"You have beautiful breasts," Amanda said, and filled her hands with them. She rubbed Marcel's nipples with her thumbs and then lowered her head to take the right one into her mouth.

Marcel's body immediately begged for more, and Amanda proved to be accommodating. She urged Marcel onto the bed and then covered Marcel's body with hers. Amanda's in-sync kisses were hot and magical, and Marcel forgot who and where she was for the moment. It surprised her that she felt so good so quickly; Amanda knew what she was doing and got right down to it. The stimulation was direct and focused. The merging of their bodies brought on an exquisite heat that steadily crescendoed into orgasm at a delightful rate. Marcel cried out as she came, and then pulled Amanda's sweat-coated body even closer to her. It was fabulous, and Marcel felt another surge of emotion as Amanda slowly worked Marcel's thigh between her legs and then started grinding herself against her. Marcel captured a swaying breast in her mouth, causing Amanda's movement to increase into a moaning symphony of *oh*'s. Amanda came hard again and collapsed on top of her like a sweet-smelling rag doll. Marcel held her and kissed her forehead until Amanda fell asleep.

Thirty minutes later, Marcel disentangled herself from Amanda, put on a robe, and went downstairs. Sex had always been the one thing that could guarantee insomnia for her. It usually took her several hours to come down from the physical high her body went through.

She had slipped out of bed so that her tossing and turning wouldn't be so disruptive. Apparently sex had the complete opposite effect on Amanda, as it did on nearly everyone else.

Marcel wasn't sure she could've gotten Amanda awake if she had wanted to.

Marcel smiled when she saw their clothes tossed all over the living room. After neatly folding them, she set out to work on the ad in the other room, but before she got too far into it, the telephone rang.

"Hi. Did I wake you?" Cricket asked.

"No," Marcel said as a flash of guilt zapped her.

"Good. I need to talk. I think this one likes playing games."

"This one? What are you talking about?"

"Naomi! Who do you think?"

"Oh."

"We were out at that new club tonight, and we're dancing and laughing and then outta the blue she starts asking me questions about you. Were we ever lovers? Do you like younger women? Are you seeing anyone right now? On and on and on until I'm *totally* outta the mood."

Marcel rolled her eyes. "And you're calling me because . . . ?"

"I'm calling for your opinion," Cricket said. "So what do you think? She has to know the score here; so is Naomi messing with me? Or is it just that she's dumb as a rock?"

"I know nothing about her," Marcel said, "so what good is my opinion?"

"Let me hear it anyway. I know you've got one."

Marcel sighed. "She's not dumb, by any means. Quite the contrary, in fact. She's bright and kind of interesting, I think."

"Of course you would think that!" Cricket reasoned. "She's been panting after you ever since that night of miniature golf."

Marcel refrained from mentioning how Cricket and Naomi had held hands at the theater earlier that evening. No evidence of panting there.

"So forget it," Cricket said. "I'm not fixing you two up. I've got my eye on her."

"How many women at a time can you —"

"Three," Cricket said with a chuckle. "I take vitamins."

"What kind?"

Cricket's laughter made Marcel smile.

"I'm thinking maybe she's just stringing me along," Cricket said. "Whatever interest she's shown in you, there's been no follow-through. She's trying to get my goat. It's obvious that you're not interested in her, so she thinks it's safe to play this game. Or maybe she's just using you to make me jealous. And it's working to a point."

Marcel let it drop. Pursuing this line of reasoning wasn't worth the aggravation.

"Okay," Cricket said. "I just wanted your thoughts on this. Thanks. Get some sleep, eh? I'll talk to you tomorrow."

With a click, Cricket was gone. Marcel hung up the phone, but before she had time to feel too guilty about talking to Cricket while Amanda was upstairs in her bed, Marcel heard rustling in the hallway. Amanda came into the dining room with nothing but a sheet wrapped around her.

"There you are," she said sleepily. "Who was on the phone?"

Marcel laughed at the adorable sight and held her arms out. Amanda opened the sheet to receive her.

"You look so cute," Marcel said, and kissed her lightly on the lips.

Amanda let go of the sheet and took Marcel's face in her hands and kissed her deeply. The tumbling in Marcel's stomach made her tremble.

"Come back to bed," Amanda whispered when they finally pulled away from each other. "I still have things I want to do to you."

"Oh," Marcel said as the fluttering began all over again.

"Lots and lots of things." Amanda tugged on the sash and opened Marcel's robe, exposing her nude body. "Or I can start right here and we can go back to bed later for the finale."

Marcel was speechless, but her body was responding.

"On the table," Amanda ordered quietly. She bundled Marcel's robe and the sheet together, making a nice cushy pillow. "Right here," Amanda said as she patted the edge of the tabletop.

Marcel loved hearing the determination in Amanda's voice and got up on the table as she'd been instructed to do.

"Scooch forward a little," Amanda said, urging Marcel closer to the table's edge. She encouraged Marcel to lie back on the make-believe robe-sheet-pillow combination. "And these go here," she said decisively as she draped Marcel's legs over her shoulders.

Amanda started licking and gently probing Marcel with her eager tongue, engulfing Marcel with sensation almost immediately. Marcel wound her fingers through Amanda's silky blond hair. She moaned and felt hot liquid desire, incandescent and exquisite, shooting through her body. Marcel came in a rush; the release was so intense and complete that she wasn't aware when the delicate stroking finally stopped.

"Amanda," she whispered. "That was . . ." she started, and then trembled again before saying, "incredible."

Amanda kissed her lingeringly before easing Marcel's legs from her shoulders. "That's just the beginning," she said, and then helped Marcel sit up on the table's edge. "I made you come too quickly. I'll know to tease you more next time so it'll last longer." She kissed the top of Marcel's head. "For both of us."

Marcel put her limp arms around Amanda's neck and let their foreheads touch. "Next time," she said weakly.

"Yes, darling. Next time. I hope to have many, many more next times."

They got out of bed at midmorning, after having made love several more times, and had a light breakfast of cinnamon toast and coffee. Marcel had finally fallen asleep at about six, but had been awakened forty-five minutes later by Amanda's sweet kisses.

Marcel found herself still a bit dazed at having Amanda there with her. "What about Cricket?" Marcel finally asked while pouring them more coffee. "I'm supposed to see her today. I can tell her then."

"Let me talk to her first," Amanda said. "I think it'll be better that way."

"Are you sure?"

Amanda came up behind her and kissed Marcel on the back of the neck. "I'm sure."

Marcel turned around and took full advantage of their closeness. "When can I see you again?" she asked, putting her arms around her. Amanda's tongue explored Marcel's mouth slowly, sweetly as they kissed near the sink.

"Can I come over tonight?" Amanda asked.

"Of course."

"I'll call you and let you know when I'll be here."

Marcel walked with her to the front door where the kissing continued. "I need to know how it goes with Cricket," Marcel said. "Are you sure you don't want me to tell her?"

Amanda gave her one last peck on the lips. "I'll take care of it. See you tonight."

Marcel finally got to work at eleven, after having called in earlier, and came through the door whistling. She felt great — happier than she's felt in a long time.

"You sure are in a good mood," Carmen said as she poked her head out of Marcel's office. "Did you finally get some sleep?"

Marcel threw her head back and laughed. "Even less than usual."

Carmen smiled knowingly. "Then you must've gotten laid!"

Marcel rolled her eyes and imagined herself blushing. Standing in the doorway Marcel found her office in total disarray and Carmen putting a twin bed together behind the desk.

"What are you doing?" Marcel inquired.

"Your mother's orders," Carmen said, "but I agree with her. Help me with this mattress."

"My mother? When did you talk to my mother?"

"At the grand opening the other night."

There's a damn bed in my office, Marcel thought incredulously. Irritated, she asked, "What exactly did my mother say? I don't want a bed in here, for crissakes! Why didn't someone ask me?" But even as she was protesting, Marcel found herself helping to heave the mattress onto the bedframe. Carmen fished in a huge bag and pulled out a package of new, baby blue sheets. Marcel could almost see the wheels turning in her mother's head, and Marcel knew that any displeasure she felt about this had to be directed at Carmen instead of her mother.

Carmen laughed. "Roslin thinks that there might be times when you're here at work that you'll get sleepy. We measured everything and made sure there would be plenty of room for a small bed in here. She even gave me specific instructions on what kind of bedding to get." Carmen smiled as she flipped the top sheet and let it slowly float down, covering the bed. "Calm, peaceful colors," Carmen said in a hushed voice. "No Wonder Woman sheets or Pokémon sheets, but a tranquil, soothing color. I had fun doing this."

"Jesus," Marcel said, a bit embarrassed that Carmen knew so much about the sleep problem that she and her mother had spent years discussing. As an alternative to having a bed in her office, Marcel tried another approach. "Why not a nice comfortable sofa with some cushy pillows?"

"And when was the last time you fell asleep on a sofa? Never, right? She's on to you," Carmen said. "Roslin knows what works best, and a comfy sofa with cushy pillows just won't hack it."

"Okay, okay."

"She picked the bed and this particular mattress out especially for you. Even the pillows. But she ran out of time and asked me to buy the sheets and get it all set up and ready."

Marcel again was able to imagine her mother in a store somewhere that specialized in beds . . . imagined her trying out each mattress in the store until she found one that met her approval. "It must be nice to know everything," Marcel said grumpily. *So much for my good mood,* she thought.

"Hey, I don't argue with your mother," Carmen said. "And neither will you."

"I know," Marcel said, resigning herself to the fact that there would be a bed in her office.

"She's right much too often for either of us to question her judgment or suggestions."

"I know, I know," Marcel said. She watched as Carmen finished making the bed with sharp, military corners and creases on the top sheet, enclosing the mattress in a light blue envelope of cotton. "Did you miss the part of my mother's speech where she explained how to make the bed for a sleep-deprived person?"

Carmen stepped back and admired her handiwork. "What's wrong with the way I made the bed?"

"It's not user friendly."

Carmen smiled and nodded. "Oh. I get it." She pulled the top sheet off and shook it out again, letting it drift down slowly to cover the bed. "Loose and inviting. Got it."

Chapter Ten

Marcel supervised the loading of their delivery truck, and Carmen and two of her brothers got the furniture in the back according to how it all needed to be unloaded for each delivery. Carmen had gotten them a sweet deal with one of the older hotels downtown to furnish several of its sitting areas with various antiques. As a result of that transaction, the Antique Villa had sold more in one day than they'd expected to sell in three months. Money was beginning to roll in.

After the last piece was carefully placed on the truck, Carmen jumped down and dusted her pants off. Her blue denim shirt still had that fresh-from-the-cleaners look to it, and her neatly cut, thick black hair showed signs of dampness near her collar.

"Is that clipboard heavy?" Carmen asked Marcel with a teasing grin.

Marcel chuckled and checked off the last thing on the invoice. "Next time, you can do this part, and I'll schlep the furniture."

"Inventory is low," Carmen said. "Time for you to go shopping again or clean out your attic."

The go-shopping part has been one of the key factors in attracting Marcel to this business venture. She found going to estate sales, flea markets, thrift shops, and other antique stores with someone else's checkbook appealing. She knew antiques and the pricing game, and the challenge of getting something for nothing made her eager to get started.

"I'll check the attic tonight," Marcel said, referring to the countless furniture pieces that had been stored in her attic over the years. That had also been a factor in opening the shop.

About an hour later, Cricket came in and pretended to browse while Marcel took care of a customer. Marcel became nervous the minute she saw her, wondering what Cricket's reaction had been to Amanda's revelation about their night together. With Marcel having spent the majority of the afternoon thinking about Amanda, she also wondered if she'd ever be able to associate her dining table with anything other than sexual bliss.

"So," Marcel said when the other customer finally left. "Did you see Amanda today?"

"Yes," Cricket said. "We had a late lunch."

She's pretty calm, Marcel thought suspiciously. She waited a moment, expecting Cricket to comment on what Amanda had told her. "And?" Marcel said finally.

"And what?" Cricket replied, puzzled.

"What did she say?"

Cricket raised an eyebrow. "About what?"

It finally became clear to Marcel that Amanda hadn't

mentioned *anything* about last night to Cricket. Marcel was torn between telling and not telling her.

"About *what*?" Cricket said again.

Marcel shifted uneasily. She hated having put herself in this position. *She's my friend. Omigod! She's my friend! What have I done?*

"Marcel," Cricket said as she snapped her fingers like a hypnotist in front of Marcel's face. "What's the matter with you?"

"Uh . . . it's about Amanda," Marcel said as her heart raced. "Last night." She had to tell her. There was no way Marcel could let this deception continue. Her relationship with Cricket thrived on honesty, no matter how painful it was. And Marcel realized now that she couldn't depend on Amanda to help with this.

"What about last night?"

"Uh . . . Amanda and I were together. We made love last night."

Now it was Cricket's turn to blink dumbly. "What?" she said, cocking her head in order to hear her better.

"Amanda and I," Marcel said as her heart sank. "Last night . . . we made love last night." She couldn't speak any louder. "And she was supposed to tell you that at lunch today."

"You and Amanda? *My* Amanda?"

"Yes," Marcel said. "Amanda."

"No way."

"I wanted to tell you myself, but she —"

"No way! *My* Amanda?"

Apparently the look on Marcel's face convinced her otherwise.

"You bitch!" Cricket hissed as she snatched her backpack and stormed toward the door.

"Cricket!" Marcel called, but decided against following her. "Damn," she mumbled. "That didn't go well."

Marcel found Amanda's business card near the phone and

dialed the number. The moment Amanda answered, Marcel began talking. "You said you would tell her."

There was a hesitation, and then Amanda said, "Marcel?"

"This morning you said you would tell her, Amanda. You knew I was seeing her today."

"And I will tell her."

"Will?" Marcel said. "I expected you to do it *today*! At lunch!"

"Today? You mean just blurt it out over a chef's salad? This is going to take time."

"Not anymore," Marcel said. "She just flew out of here like she had a rocket up her butt. I can't believe you didn't tell her. You said you would talk to her today."

"So she knows? Damn it, Marcel!"

"You said you would talk to her!"

"I *did* talk to her! But not about that! I can't believe you did this. I've gotta go."

Amanda hung up in Marcel's ear, dissolving whatever good feelings Marcel had started the day with. She knew that it was impossible for anyone else to understand the complexities of her relationship with Cricket, and Marcel also knew that her own sense of honor was foreign to other people. Those West Point morals were still engrained in her, and as a result, she refused to be a part of anyone's lie. For Marcel to keep her relationship with Amanda a secret from Cricket was out of the question for her, and Marcel assumed that Amanda had understood that when they'd discussed it before. One of the reasons Marcel and Cricket had remained so close all these years was because of their brutal honesty with each other. Marcel depended on Cricket to tell her when she needed to take things less seriously and stop being so rigid and "such an officer," while Marcel was the person who always let Cricket know when she had spinach in her teeth or when clothes looked unflattering on her. These situations were seldom pleasant, but Marcel and Cricket loved each other as only ex-lovers and true friends can, and they would continue to be vital fixtures in each other's lives. A boatload of new lovers wouldn't change that. Nothing would ever change that.

Marcel was upset and confused about Amanda's anger; she decided to let Amanda and Cricket work through a few things before she approached either of them again. Amanda stayed on her mind, and luckily for Marcel's state of mind, customers poured in and bought antiques at an alarming rate. A while later, Cricket called.

"Was she there when I talked to you last night?" she demanded.

"Yes," Marcel said after taking a deep breath.

"Why didn't you tell me then?"

"The conversation never got around to me. As usual we only talked about you."

"Oh, cute, Marcel. It's just like you to turn this thing around and make *me* the bad guy. You bitch!"

Marcel was slowly getting angry. "Then it wouldn't do me any good now to remind you that when you called me last night, it was with the sole purpose of discussing the new woman you're drooling over. Or have you forgotten that?"

"Bitch, bitch, bitch!" Cricket yelled, and then slammed the phone down.

Marcel shook her head and hung up.

"I was serious about that shopping spree," Carmen said a while later as she helped Marcel rearrange a few of the heavier pieces in the showroom. "We need new inventory now, so I'll have time to work on it and get it ready to sell."

"I'm on it," Marcel said. "I'm leaving for the Hill Country in the morning. I also heard about an old hotel in Mason that they're tearing down. Rumor control says they've got several old barns out back full of interesting things."

The door opened and another customer came in; Marcel felt her whole body emit a little groan at the sight of Jordan Wheatly.

"How about a hug?" Jordan said as she came over and gave Marcel a more than friendly squeeze. "Good to see you again, Carmen."

"Likewise."

Jordan stepped back and immediately feigned interest in an antique roll-top desk. "Big Boy's out of town, so I decided to spend some of his money."

Ah, Marcel thought. *The General's gone and she's out shopping. But not necessarily for a desk.*

"You've already got more furniture than you know what to do with," Marcel said, hoping to sound amiable but not interested.

Jordan looked at her with mischief in her eyes and said, "There's always room for more. You know how I like having a little something extra." She thumped the price tag with the outrageously high figure on it and said, "I'll take it." She turned and asked Marcel when she could deliver it.

"This afternoon or early in the morning," Marcel said.

"Then I'd prefer this afternoon." Jordan whipped out her checkbook and started writing. With a familiar wicked grin she said, "And wear exactly what you have on. I like that pseudo-rugged look on you. It's quite effective and very becoming."

"Excuse me?" Marcel said. "I won't be delivering it."

Jordan stopped her pen in midair over the check. "Marcel," she said with that bored tone that Marcel found so annoying. That bored general's-wife tone. "This is a sizable purchase I'm making."

"And you're buying a desk only," Marcel informed her, and then with added emphasis said, "Only. The desk *only.*"

"It's just a simple little request," Jordan said innocently.

She finished writing the check and ripped it out of the checkbook. With a smile she said, "We could have a nice dinner there in Mamie Eisenhower's house."

Marcel sighed. She already knew exactly what would happen. Within two minutes of her arrival, they would be kissing and Marcel would once again end up being the voice of reason.

"You know I can't," Marcel said.

"At first it was because you outranked me," Jordan said, "and then it was because Big Boy was your boss. Well, none of that applies now, Marcel, so what's stopping us from having a little fun together?"

"He's still your husband. I don't need a complication like that in my life." *And there's no telling who else you've been with lately,* Marcel thought with a shudder.

"You can be so self-righteous sometimes, Marcel. I hate my life." She recapped her pen and tossed it in her purse. "So what does it take to get fucked these days?"

Marcel laughed and didn't have an answer for her. "How many times have I told you that it's very unbecoming for the General's wife to use the *F* word?"

"Fuck, fuck fuck," Jordan said with gusto. "Can I use your fucking phone, please?"

Marcel motioned toward the telephone beside them on the counter.

"Do you have one with more privacy?"

Marcel nodded. "Back there in my office."

Jordan came around the counter and Marcel opened the office door for her. Jordan's eyes went directly to the bed behind Marcel's desk.

"Hmm," she said playfully. "So you *were* expecting me."

"The phone's on the desk," Marcel said.

"We could have such fun together, Marcel, if you'd just lighten up a little." Jordan casually dialed a number. "Me and you. Alone. With Big Boy away." She smiled and then winked. "Me and you in Mamie Eisenhower's house. Just think of the possibilities."

Marcel shook her head and wondered if Jordan would ever change. She closed the door and left her alone with the phone.

When Jordan finally departed, Carmen came out of the work area in the back, smelling of lemon oil and sawdust. It was a combination that Marcel was getting familiar with and finding that it was comforting in many ways.

"I figure if we could have all your girlfriends buy something from us occasionally, we'd be in business forever," Carmen said with a teasing wink.

Marcel rolled her eyes and stated simply that she had no girlfriends. Amanda hadn't called. Cricket hadn't called. She wondered what was going on with those two. She was gradually coming to the conclusion that a reconciliation of sorts was probably in the works for them.

"So how are you doing?" Carmen asked. "I mean really?"

Marcel took a deep breath and shrugged. "You mean other than feeling life a fool? I'm fine."

"You're not a fool," Carmen said. "The bigger fools are the women who hurt you. I'm here if you need to talk."

"I know. Thanks."

The front door opened again, and they both looked up as Naomi came in. Marcel's eyes widened in surprise at seeing her, and she resisted the urge to thump Carmen when she heard her say, "If we could just get each of them to buy something."

Chapter Eleven

Marcel was usually able to read people fairly well, but Naomi had a tendency to confuse her. The only real information that Marcel had to go on was Cricket's view of this woman, which was more than likely distorted into a caricature of who Naomi really was. Marcel did, however, see something there that she liked, even though she wasn't exactly sure what it was. The word *charisma* came to mind, and she acknowledged the fact that Naomi had it. Marcel found her attractive but felt a little uneasy admitting that.

Carmen, who was back in the work area already, had left shaking her head and chuckling. Marcel wasn't sure what was going on with Naomi at that particular moment, but she knew which approach she wanted to take with her to help clarify things.

"It's nice to see you again," Marcel said. "Can I help you find something?"

Naomi's smile was warm and friendly. "I saw a small table the other night that I liked very much." She glanced around the showroom but apparently didn't see what she was looking for. "This is the first chance I've had to get back here since the grand opening."

"Business has been good," Marcel said. "We've probably sold the table you were interested in. Where was it sitting that night?"

Naomi described the table and where it had been. "I can see now that I should've gotten it then."

"I know the table you're talking about, and I can keep an eye out for a similar one."

"Would you? Thanks."

Marcel returned to the counter and made a note on an index card, then had Naomi write her name and phone number on the bottom of the card.

"I don't suppose you're free for dinner tonight," Naomi said nonchalantly as she scribbled.

Marcel was caught by pleasant surprise and didn't know what to say at first. The remote possibility of seeing Amanda later, in addition to having to work on the ad she hadn't finished yet, popped into her head.

"Tonight isn't good for me," Marcel said. Then with a pang of irritation, she remembered sitting beside Naomi in the theater last night while Cricket held Naomi's hand in the dark.

"How about tomorrow?" Naomi asked.

Marcel liked her persistence and was beginning to think that maybe Cricket and Carmen were right about Naomi's interest in her.

"I'm out of town tomorrow," Marcel said, and to soften the

rejection a little, she smiled and added, "but I might find the table you're looking for then. You never know."

"May I call you?" Naomi asked. There was determination in her eyes instead of the disappointment Marcel had expected to find there. It was the first time they'd actually looked at each other, and Marcel knew right away what Cricket found so attractive about her — the spray of dark curls and the flash of perfect white teeth that had more than likely cost her parents a bundle. Her features were pleasant; she would never be glamorous or what most people would call beautiful, but Marcel liked Naomi.

Cricket, Marcel thought suddenly. *This is Cricket's newest infatuation. And she's here asking me for a date.*

"I'd like to get together with you sometime," Naomi continued. "I hope you don't mind me saying this, but I find you very interesting. Our lives are so different, and the things you've done fascinate me."

Marcel felt her face glowing and decided to put this entire conversation in perspective for both of them. "You realize, of course, that Cricket is my friend," Marcel said.

"I know."

"And you also realize that Cricket is interested in you."

Naomi shrugged. "She has Amanda."

"She had Amanda when you started seeing her."

"I'm not 'seeing' her. We work together."

"Are you not aware that Cricket wants more than that from you?"

"I know I'm never quite sure how to handle her," Naomi admitted. "Open relationships are foreign to me, and I have no point of reference for a lot of what Cricket does."

"I think it's something new for Cricket, too."

Naomi sighed. "I think it's only fair that I tell you why I'm putting up with Cricket's teasing and overall nonsense. Keeping a connection with Cricket gives me an opportunity to see you. I think you're one of the most intriguing women I've ever met. I'm trying my best to get my feelings across to Cricket, but she's not really listening to me. One minute I'm sure she understands exactly what I'm saying, and the next minute it's like she has amnesia."

Marcel smiled and arched an eyebrow at hearing the word *intriguing*. It wasn't a word she was accustomed to hearing in reference to herself. Being a female with rank in the Army, the more traditional word *bitch* was what she was used to. And Cricket seemed to have adopted that particular word for her as well.

"Then why were you holding Cricket's hand during the movie last night if you find me so intriguing?"

"You saw that?" Naomi asked, horrified.

"I saw it and Amanda saw it."

Naomi, who had now turned red, closed her eyes and took a deep breath. "I couldn't believe she did that. Did you also notice that I kept my hands in my lap the rest of the night after it happened?" She nervously ran her fingers through her curls and seemed younger than she had a few moments ago. "I like Cricket as a friend. It's nice having someone so full of energy and mischief in a work environment. But that's all there is to it for me. I'm sorry that you saw something that gave you another impression."

Marcel had to admit that Cricket was the one painting a different picture of the situation.

"Cricket is interested in you, and she's my friend." Marcel refrained from adding, *Since I slept with her lover last night it seems like a good idea not to get involved with you, too.*

Naomi's painful expression caught Marcel off guard, and it occurred to her for the first time that this whole thing might mean a lot more to Naomi than Marcel had originally thought. *After all,* Marcel thought, *hasn't Cricket been complaining about Naomi's interest in me all along?*

"That's not what I wanted to hear," Naomi said.

"Cricket's feelings for you, whatever they may be, haven't changed."

Naomi looked at her for a moment and then said, "Don't hold me responsible for Cricket's feelings." Naomi managed a weak smile. "I can see that I have my work cut out for me here. You haven't seen the last of me."

As she turned to go, Marcel felt a twinge of regret. *How does Cricket find these wonderful women?* she wondered. *How does she ever keep them straight?*

Marcel got home late and had no messages on her answering machine. Amanda's silence was pretty much saying it all — their time together had consisted of only one night. That was obvious now, and Marcel reminded herself that she needed to get over it.

To take her mind off Amanda, Marcel foraged through the attic to see what was there and what could be taken to the shop the next day. For several items, she would have to do some research on the current market value, but she had an idea what the majority of the pieces would sell for. Most had been won in poker games over the years, and Roslin had told her more than once to take anything that she wanted.

After getting an idea about what she wanted to take to the shop the next day, Marcel called Carmen and made arrangements to have it all picked up first thing in the morning. It was after nine when she finally settled down to concentrate on the ad that was due on Monday, and once those finishing touches were completed, she snatched up the ringing phone beside her.

"Good," Roslin said, "I didn't wake you."

Marcel sighed. She had hoped that it would be Amanda, but she was glad to hear her mother's voice, too.

"Are you winning?" Marcel asked.

"I lost Key West again. It's time for a break. I'll be home tomorrow afternoon."

Marcel laughed and shook her head. Her mother treated

property like it was part of a Monopoly game — cashing in Baltimore Avenue to pay for a railroad. The Key West property had already been recycled three times in the last two years, and it was obvious to Marcel that her mother needed to find a new circle of people to gamble with.

"I'll be out of town tomorrow," Marcel said. "I'm going shopping for antiques. Shall I ask Carmen to pick you up at the airport?"

"I'll find my way," Roslin said. "See you tomorrow."

"Try and cheer up some, will you? This place is like a tomb already."

"Can't promise anything. Dipping into Key West took care of that. Toodles, and get some sleep."

As Marcel hung up the phone, she wondered what Amanda was doing right then. She had spent a good part of the day trying not to think about her, but now that she was home and sitting at the very table where Amanda had made love to her that morning, the memory of those precious few hours they'd spent together was sharp and painful. Marcel wanted to call Amanda just to hear her voice, but she also needed to know what exactly had happened with Cricket earlier that day. Marcel wanted something a bit more definite than her own suspicions about what their time together had meant to Amanda. After having spent the majority of her life in a very rigid, disciplined environment where doing what was best for her wasn't always the objective, Marcel wanted specifics when it came to matters of the heart.

Crossing her arms on the table, she rested her head there for just a moment. When she finally woke up, it was two in the morning. Amanda hadn't called.

Carmen and one of her brothers arrived at seven-thirty, and between the three of them, they got what they wanted out of the attic and loaded onto the truck. Marcel followed them to the shop where they unloaded everything into Carmen's work area in the back. Marcel wiped the sweat from her brow on the sleeve of her beige oxford shirt and wondered why she'd bothered taking a shower before doing all the lifting and arranging in the early morning Texas heat.

Carmen held the truck keys out to her. "Shop till you drop, Colonel. I even gassed it up for you already."

Marcel smiled. She liked the way Carmen was forever taking care of those small details that Marcel disliked tending to.

"I'll have my cell phone on in case you need me," Marcel said. "Or in case I get any calls." She still held out some hope that Amanda would get in touch with her again.

"Which one of the three are you waiting to hear from?" Carmen asked. "The General's wife or one of Cricket's girlfriends?"

The comment was like a slap in the face. Marcel snatched the keys from her and scowled her displeasure. Having had it put to her so bluntly, Marcel cringed as she thought about her behavior over the last few days.

"I appreciate the support," Marcel said sarcastically.

"All I'm saying is that you can do better. It amazes me how these women find you," Carmen said as her own disbelief and irritation surfaced. "I know you. I've seen how you struggle with their perceptions of you." Shaking her head she added, "You're like a magnet for lesbian weirdos."

"Again," Marcel said, "thanks for your support." She got in the huge truck and drove out of the parking lot on her way to rescue old furniture. In the rearview mirror, Marcel could see Carmen standing in the parking lot with her hands on her hips, staring after her.

Marcel had the truck's air conditioner wide open and blowing on her face to ensure that she stayed awake. Now was not the time to get sleepy. She enjoyed the drive to the Hill Country and stopped at every little one-room flea market along the way. So far all she'd found was an oak bed frame that was a steal.

Even as a child, Marcel had loved shopping and experiencing the thrill of finding a bargain. Her mother had instilled in her a respect for money at an early age, and from day one had been amused at her daughter's frugal nature when it came to making a purchase. Marcel had a keen eye for quality and workmanship, and an interest in the unusual. She and Carmen were practical and agreed on many things, which made them good business partners, but they also shared a true appreciation for anything made of wood. Marcel's passion came from saving old desks and chairs, rescuing them and bringing them to Carmen, who would in turn give them a facelift and a new life of their own.

As Marcel sped down the highway, she thought about the desk Jordan had purchased the day before. Each furniture piece in their shop had its own Robicheaux-Morales history, and Marcel remembered finding that particular desk at an auction in Tacoma last summer. She wondered where Jordan would put it in Mamie Eisenhower's house, and if it would be used or just dusted by the maid. There were times when Marcel felt like the coordinator for a furniture adoption agency, with her goal being to find good homes for each piece.

As she began winding down a bit more, she let herself reflect on Jordan, too. Now that Marcel was officially retired and General Wheatly was no longer her boss, the prospect of maintaining a friendship with Jordan was more feasible, but Marcel wasn't sure that she wanted to. Jordan could give her a good workout on the tennis court, but Jordan would probably always come through with innuendos and attempted stolen kisses when they were alone together. Jordan's smoldering sexuality had no true outlet. A husband plus a lover might not even be enough for her. Marcel often wondered if Jordan had any friends whom she hadn't tried to sleep with. In several ways Marcel felt sorry for her, even though Jordan chose to stay in an unsatisfying marriage. She knew she would have to make certain things very clear to Jordan, and draw a line that couldn't be crossed, if a friendship was to work. Marcel wasn't sure that Jordan was up to that. Marcel recognized that Jordan and Cricket were so much alike that it was almost scary.

Marcel remembered her stint in Germany with Jordan and the time the hospital was faced with being over budget for the last quarter of the fiscal year. Marcel had called a meeting of all departments in the hospital, and then-First Lieutenant Jordan McGowen was there representing the department of nursing. The conference room had been full as Marcel proceeded to tell everyone what the money situation was. As in most budget meetings, representatives were unwilling to curtail their expenses. The arguments had become heated, and there were bitter accusations about Marcel's commitment to patient care. At one point, Jordan came to Marcel's defense in a surprisingly eloquent bottom-line summation of the facts--there was no money, and they'd simply have to make the most of the resources available.

After Jordan's brief spiel, Marcel noticed that the other departmental representatives stopped taking so personally what Marcel had been saying. Jordan had somehow reached them. Marcel also noticed the way Jordan looked at her immediately afterward, ready with a smile and what Marcel would later learn was a sensual habit of slowly moistening her lips with the tip of her tongue.

A few days after the budget meeting, Marcel had found herself on an elevator in the hospital where the next stop blessed her with twenty or so soldiers in full field gear, with Lieutenant Jordan McGowen leading the way. Everyone was packed in like thrifty tourists on a free bus, with no allowance for personal space. It quickly had become a let's-see-how-many-people-we-can-stuff-in-an-elevator game. Marcel, unfortunately, had been pushed toward the back, with Jordan somehow again directly behind her in the corner. There was no room to move, and Marcel felt Marcel's hands firmly planted on her ass, rubbing slowly and suggestively. Then Marcel felt hands on her hips, pulling her back even closer so that Jordan's breasts pressed against her. Marcel was immediately aroused — and annoyed at the way her body was responding. The fear of getting caught was real, even though no one paid any attention to them as the chatter in the elevator escalated. The elevator stopped on every floor before finally reaching Marcel's floor, where several people got out to let her through. Marcel, aware that Jordan had followed her, unlocked the door to her office and knew exactly what she should do — chastise Jordan for her behavior and strongly hint at the possibility of disciplinary action if such a thing were to ever happen again.

Yes, Marcel thought now as she dodged a deer carcass in the road. *That's what I should've done then.*

As soon as Marcel had her office door unlocked and opened, Jordan slipped in behind her and pulled Marcel into her arms and kissed her. Again Marcel's body reacted in a way that infuriated her.

"Take this off," Jordan whispered as she tugged on the buttons of Marcel's uniform. She randomly kissed Marcel's cheek and mouth and said, "I've got fifteen minutes before I'm on call. God, you've got the nicest ass." Her left hand was on Marcel again, rubbing and pulling her closer while Jordan continued to fumble with the buttons on Marcel's uniform with her other hand.

Marcel gritted her teeth and said, "What the *hell* are you doing?"

"What does it look like I'm doing," Jordan said as she nuzzled Marcel's neck.

Marcel abruptly stepped away from her and straightened her uniform. Jordan's flagrant aggression was a definite warning for Marcel. The stories about entrapment, witch hunts, set-ups, and being let go from the service were true and scary. Had Jordan been a little less desperate and pushy, and not a bisexual, Marcel might have been more receptive to her advances, but none of that was the case. Marcel was suspicious of Jordan's motives and leery of her actions. Marcel reached around her for the handle on the door and opened it, saying simply, "Out."

"Oh sure," Jordan said with a confident laugh. She pushed the door closed again. "Are you trying to tell me you don't want this too?"

Marcel was not going to discuss this with her, and she was furious for allowing herself to be put in such a position.

"We're two consenting adults and both officers."

I don't know you, Marcel thought, *and there's no way I'm going to get involved with someone this careless.*

"The Army has no sense of humor when it comes to homosexual behavior, Lieutenant. I've worked too hard to throw it all away on a cheap thrill in an elevator or a quickie in my office." She opened the door again and took Jordan by the elbow. "Out," she said. With a little shove, Jordan was in the hallway again.

"And she hasn't changed a bit," Marcel said out loud as she slowed down for a flea market entrance. Shopping would cheer her up considerably.

Chapter Twelve

Marcel pulled the truck into her winding driveway and met Cricket's car coming out. Marcel stopped and rolled down her window, but Cricket waved an angry middle finger at her and kept going.

Okay fine, Marcel thought, and reluctantly understood Cricket's unwillingness to speak with her. *Amanda was her girlfriend*, she reminded herself again, and then amended the thought by saying out loud, "*Is* her girlfriend."

She drove into the outrageously large eight-car garage that held many of her mother's vehicles, which were traded on a regular basis when the card games were local in nature. Marcel locked the doors and the back of the truck, making sure that the cache of furniture she'd spent the day finagling from dealers was secure. Marcel reasoned that the truck would be safer here at home than sitting in the parking lot at the shop.

She was dusty and hungry, and anxious to know why Cricket had been there. *Maybe she left a note for me or something,* Marcel thought. It had been awhile since either of them had expressed this type of anger at the other; but over the years they'd taken turns aggravating each other, and it was Cricket's turn to be on the receiving end of it this time.

"There you are," Roslin said as she came out of the kitchen drying her hands on an apron. It always made Marcel smile when she caught her mother in an uncharacteristically domestic moment. Had she not known already that her mother had lost Key West, the wearing of an apron alone would have told Marcel that Roslin's trip had not been a good one.

"I'm all dusty from rummaging in barns today," Marcel warned as Roslin came over to hug her.

"Then go take a shower. Dinner will be ready in about fifteen minutes."

"What was Cricket doing here?"

"We'll talk about it over dinner."

Marcel went into her bedroom and felt a wave of emotion the moment she saw her bed — the place she and Amanda had made love. She pulled open drawers and found clean clothes, and knew that she wouldn't be able to sleep there that night.

The shower felt good, and Marcel suddenly was quite tired. If she could just get her mind to shut down for a few minutes, she'd be able to sleep soon.

She went downstairs and saw the table in the dining room set for two and realized that if she couldn't sleep in her bed later, then she damn well couldn't eat on the table where Amanda had made love to her. She picked up the two place settings and carried them into the kitchen.

"Can we eat in here?"

"Sure, baby," Roslin said. "Sit down. You look tired."

Roslin set a dish of some sort of Hamburger Helper concoction on the kitchen table and got a salad from the refrigerator.

"I thought I hid all the hamburger box things better than that," Marcel said, teasing her. The casserole smelled delicious.

"Under the sink next to the bug spray. Now eat up. You'll love it."

Roslin's laughter never failed to make Marcel's mood improve. When Marcel was in high school and Roslin would return from a brief gambling trip, Marcel could always tell how her mother had done by the first meal they consumed immediately upon her arrival. If Roslin had won, then they would pick up Cricket and go for steak. If she had lost, then there would be something containing hamburger on the table. And it didn't matter what else was in the house to eat; hamburger was the meal of choice after a financial loss.

"So," Roslin said as she dished out healthy scoops of noodles with chunks of ground beef clinging to it. "What possessed you to sleep with your best friend's lover?"

Marcel set her fork down and sighed heavily. *So much for my appetite,* she thought.

"Cricket is very upset."

"I know she is," Marcel said. "And she has every right to be."

"Tell me what happened."

"But was she as upset as I was the time she told Jimmy Sodastrum I'd started my period?"

Roslin closed her eyes and chuckled. "She's a different kind of upset than you were then, dear."

Marcel sighed again. "I know."

"She doesn't want to see you right now, even though she came here specifically to see you."

"I'll wait until she cools down a little, and then I'll call her." Marcel picked up her fork again.

"You still haven't told me what happened," Roslin reminded her.

Marcel explained how the four of them had gone out, and how she had come home after the movie. "Then Amanda showed up here."

"When did you call her?" Roslin asked.

"When did I call who?"

"Amanda."

"I didn't call Amanda."

"Cricket said that she was out with Amanda and a friend when Amanda got a call on her cell phone. At the time Cricket didn't know who it was, but Amanda says it was you."

Marcel was stunned. She blinked several times and looked at her mother again. "Amanda told Cricket that I called her?"

"That's what Cricket says."

Marcel had absolutely no appetite now and suddenly felt very tired. *Why would Cricket lie about that,* she wondered. *Cricket is a lot of things, but she's not a liar.*

"So you didn't call Amanda," Roslin said gently.

Marcel closed her eyes and swallowed against that familiar lump in her throat. "No. I didn't call Amanda."

"Then tell me what happened."

"It doesn't matter what happened."

"It matters to Cricket."

"I assume they're back together," Marcel said, her voice low and brimming with emotion.

"It's my understanding they've never been apart. Except for the night Amanda was here."

Marcel nodded, folded up her napkin, and set it beside her untouched salad. "I'm going to bed. I'll be in the guest room."

"Marcel," Roslin said as she reached for her daughter's hand. "I'm praying to the goddess that you're not in love with Amanda. You deserve better than this."

Marcel squeezed her mother's hand. "Ya think?"

~ ~ ~ ~ ~

When sleep finally came, Marcel dreamed about furniture — finding it, haggling over it, buying it, loading it, unloading it, watching Carmen transform it into something more quaint and useful than it had been in its original condition. Furniture, furniture, furniture — desks, chairs, tables, beds. All night long, Marcel kept loading it in the truck, piece after piece, as though the truck were actually a never-ending tunnel shaped like a truck, and no matter how many things she put into it, there was always room for more. But there had also been something else that had captured Marcel's attention in her dream. Now that she was lying on her back in bed, staring at the ceiling in the guest room, she remembered hands . . . nice, sensitive hands . . . remembered watching them as they touched a cheek. Capable hands that cared about what they were doing. Hands that would soothe and mend, heal and explore.

Marcel woke up a little more as she lay there. A low-wattage light was on across the room; she guessed her mother had turned a lamp on for her before going to bed herself. Marcel reached over and picked up her watch on the nightstand. It was three A.M., and she'd gotten almost five hours of sleep.

I wonder how long it'll be before Cricket calls me, she thought. The longest they'd ever stayed angry with each other had been four days, and that incident had also involved a woman — a female West Point cadet and classmate of Marcel's who had fallen for Cricket during one of Cricket's many visits to New York. But for now, Marcel didn't know what to do about Amanda. It was clear to her now that Amanda hadn't been in love with her, although Marcel would've been well on her way had the circumstances been a little different. *But Amanda lied to me,* Marcel thought. *Lied about wanting to tell Cricket about us, and lied to Cricket about the phone call.* More than anything, Marcel felt saddened by what had happened. Amanda wasn't the person Marcel had thought she was, but that didn't comfort her.

She got up, dressed, and went downstairs, knowing that she wouldn't be able to sleep again. *Five hours*, she thought with a smile as she found the rest of her salad in the refrigerator where her mother had put it just hours before.

"Nice haul," Carmen said as she climbed up into the back of the truck.

It was an overcast day with a good chance of rain later that afternoon. Low, rumbling thunder could be heard in the distance, and Marcel loved it.

"How much did it cost us?" Carmen asked as she scanned the truck's contents. There were two old desks with spider webs still clinging to them and several headboards made of cherry or oak. The remaining pieces were various claw-footed tables and an oak bookcase that had some scarring on one side.

"Two thousand for the works," Marcel said. "The headboards alone will bring twice that."

"I'm thinking you're right," Carmen said. She unwrapped a heavy blanket from a small table and carefully handed it down to Marcel. "So did you have fun?"

Marcel smiled. "You know I did."

"Who helped you load all this stuff?"

"I hired two high-school boys who were mowing grass next door." Marcel quietly thanked Carmen a hundred times for insisting that they pay the extra and get a truck with a lift on it. "Did I get any calls while I was gone?"

"Jordan," Carmen said.

"Nothing from Cricket or Amanda?"

"No, just Jordan. And she sounded a bit distracted, but with her it's hard to really tell."

"Maybe the General came home and found out how much she spent on the desk."

They got the truck unloaded and everything spread out in

119

Carmen's workshop area. The pieces that Marcel had gotten from the barn sale in Mason were spider infested. Occasionally she heard Carmen cut loose with some colorful Spanish, which was always followed by loud stomping noises.

If buying old furniture was Marcel's passion, then cleaning it up after its purchase ran a close second. After the initial spiders and rodent droppings were adequately taken care of, she liked checking the old desks for anything that had been left behind by a previous owner. In the past, she'd found Indian-head pennies, old postage stamps, love letters, postcards, and antique fountain pens. Some furniture pieces would only need to be wiped down and cleaned properly, while others would need to have more attention.

"A little lemon oil on this one and it'll be fine," Carmen said as she stepped back and gave a small end table her full attention. "Did you have any problems while you were gone? Did you find places you'd like to go back to?"

Marcel nodded. "I was in heaven. See that oak headboard? I battled a nest of hornets for it."

"I would've left it."

"And that's why I don't take you with me."

They worked on their new acquisitions into the late afternoon in between handling customers and answering the phone. Curious people from the neighborhood were still dropping by to check them out, and the usual rush of customers during the day kept Marcel on the run. They were busiest on the weekends and in the afternoons when people were on their way home from work, but there was still a steady flow of customers most of the day.

Marcel had just finished rubbing lemon oil on the oak headboard when she heard the door ding, announcing the arrival of more customers. She went to greet them, wiping her hands on a soft, clean rag, and found Cricket in the showroom, wide-eyed and pale.

"Hi," Marcel said quietly. She was glad to see her and relieved that they would finally get everything out in the open. Cricket's expression, however, didn't relay the anger that Marcel had expected to see there. "Hey," Marcel said. "Are you okay?"

"Your mother," Cricket mumbled. Her eyes were the size of walnuts, and Cricket was so upset that Marcel immediately thought the worst.

Her heart began to pound, and a paralyzing fear overcame her as Marcel was barely able to utter, "What's happened to my mother?"

"Your mother," Cricket muttered again. "I . . . oh, Jesus. I kissed her. I . . ."

Marcel blinked rapidly a few times and then turned her head as though trying to tune Cricket's voice in better. "What?" Marcel said. She knew that she'd misunderstood her. "Is my mother okay? When did you see her last?"

"I just came from your house."

"Was my mother all right?"

"Yes," Cricket said. "Your mother is fine. She's incredible, in fact. My god, Marcel. I *kissed* her!"

That same wide-eyed, shocked expression had returned, which made Marcel stop and finally listen to what Cricket was saying.

"You kissed her," Marcel repeated as her heart rate began to return to normal. Her mother wasn't dying. Cricket was just being silly and scaring her on purpose. She allowed herself to be angry now that she knew her mother was okay. "Kissed her how?"

Cricket's eyes brimmed with tears and fear. "A lips-parted-tongue-in-her-mouth kiss. A *kiss* kiss!"

It was now Marcel's turn to mimic the wide-eyed look. "A *kiss* kiss?" Her nose curled up a little at the thought of what Cricket was suggesting.

"But that's not the part that has me so —"

"You kissed my mother?" Marcel said incredulously. "Are you bullshitting me?"

"As God is my witness. I'm so serious that I think I might faint."

"Why would you do such a thing?"

"I don't know!"

Marcel was still a bit stunned at Cricket's confession. "What did she do?"

Cricket's eyes widened again. "She kissed me back!"

Marcel's short, abrupt laughter broke some of the tension. No way was she buying this. "Sure she did. Okay. What's this really all about?"

Cricket closed her eyes and visibly trembled. "She did, Marcel. As God is my —"

"I heard you the first time, Scarlet," Marcel said. "It's just that I don't believe you."

"I don't care what you believe. I need your help. What should I do now?"

"What about Amanda?" Marcel asked. Why this question was suddenly so important, she didn't have a clue.

"Amanda," Cricket repeated. Her walnut-shaped eyes suddenly became menacing slits at the reminder of Marcel's betrayal. "Oh yes. Amanda. I forgot that I wasn't speaking to you."

"So to get even with me for Amanda, you decided to kiss my mother?"

"I've waited my whole life to kiss your mother!" Cricket shot back.

"I still don't believe you."

"Forget it. Is Carmen here? I need a real friend right now."

"She's in the back. Knock yourself out."

As Cricket went through the door that led to the workshop area, Marcel reached for the phone to call her mother.

"Cricket's here," Marcel said as soon as Roslin answered. "And she's acting weirder than usual."

"Can I speak to her?" Roslin asked. Marcel could tell by her mother's voice that she was upset.

"She's with Carmen right now. I'll get her in a minute." Marcel felt her heart begin rapidly thumping again. "Tell me what happened."

"Not yet. I'm not ready to talk about it."

Omigod, it's true! She was shocked and bewildered, but knew that when she got home later she would somehow get the details out of her.

"Oh, by the way," Roslin said. Marcel had to press the phone closer to her ear as the rumble of thunder made it hard for her to hear. "General Wheatly called and left you a message."

Wanting a clarification of that statement, Marcel said, "You mean his secretary called. Generals don't know how to use a phone on their own."

"No, *he* called." Roslin laughed as she seemed to return to normal again. "And from what I remember, you forgot how to dial a phone the minute you got a secretary, so this isn't just a *general* thing. It's an *officer* thing."

"Did he say what he wanted?" Marcel asked, ignoring her as another low rumble of thunder made her listen more carefully.

"He wants you to call him," Roslin said and gave her the number. "Can I speak to Cricket now?"

"I'm worried about you."

"I know you are," Roslin said quietly. "And maybe you should be. Now let me talk to Cricket."

"Yeah, sure." Marcel stuck her head in the workshop and told Cricket she had a phone call.

Marcel was tired and went home early; Carmen volunteered to close up for her. When she left, Cricket was still on the phone with Roslin, which irritated Marcel even more.

"That's a business phone," Marcel said as she gathered a few of her things from behind the counter, unceremoniously moving Cricket out of the way.

"You've got call waiting," Cricket said as she covered the phone with her hand. "I'm taking care of things. Can I have a little privacy here?"

Marcel left and delivered the ad she'd spent days working on. She drove home with her windows down and liked the sound of thunder in the distance. The temperature had dropped about fifteen degrees into the low seventies, and weather reports on the radio were predicting storms all evening. Being from south Texas where droughts were common, she loved thunderstorms and the anticipation of rain.

When she finally got home, her mother was on the phone, and Marcel could tell that she was still talking to Cricket. A glance at her watch verified that they'd been at it for over an hour. Roslin saw her and finished her call.

"That was Cricket," she said.

"I know. What's going on? She told me what happened today."

Roslin shrugged. "I told you earlier that I'm not ready to talk about it yet."

Marcel sat on the arm of the sofa with a decisive plop. She had always confided in her mother, and Roslin's reluctance to share things with her often left Marcel confused and hurt.

"I don't know which one of us was more surprised," Roslin said after a moment. She stood next to the sofa and leaned down to kiss the top of Marcel's head. "Cricket was surprised that she had such courage, while I surprised that I responded to her so quickly." She sat down across from Marcel in an overstuffed chair.

Marcel was at a total loss for words. This was unreal, and she suddenly felt out of sync with her surroundings. She was so angry with Cricket for bringing this element into her life, and she could barely restrain herself from getting in her car and paying Cricket a little visit. Never had her mother ever made a reference to anything even closely resembling her own sexuality, so this entire incident had Marcel confused and dazed.

Marcel's father had died in an auto accident in Paris when Marcel was only a few months old. Roslin and Marcel had returned to Texas three years later when Roslin's father became ill. Armand Robicheaux, Marcel's father, left them financially secure because of his death, and Marcel's grandfather had been heavily insured as well when he finally died. Roslin had invested most of that money for Marcel and had refrained from touching it even during the hamburger years, but once Marcel was out of school and on her own, she had made wise investments and had done well in the military. Money had never been a real problem for either of them. Roslin had never remarried, and Marcel couldn't remember her ever dating. Roslin had told her once that Marcel's father had been the love of her life and that until something drastic changed, that's the way it would always be.

"Did you call the General back?" Roslin asked, cutting into Marcel's thoughts.

"No." She glanced at her watch and decided that General Wheatly had probably left his office for the day.

"I still have the number over there by the phone," Roslin said. "He was pleasant but insistent."

Marcel decided to call him and get it over with.

It was a number she wasn't familiar with, which meant that he wasn't at the office or at home. And there was no area code, so the General wasn't out of town on business. He answered immediately, and Marcel could tell that he was on a cell phone.

"Yes, General. This is Colonel Robicheaux. My mother gave me your message."

"Marcel," he grunted. "Thank you for returning my call. I have something to discuss with you. Be in my office in thirty minutes."

Two things immediately caught her attention, the first being his patronizing tone. Marcel had identified herself as "Colonel" Robicheaux, but he had chosen to call her by her first name when he addressed her. In the past during staff meetings, he would call Marcel's male colleagues who were in attendance by their rank and last name, while referring to her by her first name only. On the surface, it looked as though he knew her better than the others, when in fact he knew them all equally well. It was a power thing for him — a way to lessen her presence among her peers, a way to point out just one more time that her accomplishments or ability to achieve the rank of colonel was somehow less important than anything her male counterparts had done. Marcel's retirement subsequently gave her the freedom to finally be angry about such treatment. She was no longer willing to accept it.

Then the second thing that immediately sent her anger shooting to the surface was how he ordered her to his office. *Be in my office in thirty minutes,* she thought. *Who does he think he is?* Not only was he no longer her boss, but she was now a civilian and couldn't be ordered anywhere. *A simple* please *would've done wonders here,* she thought.

"I'm not going to your office, General. I have things to do. What is it you want? Can it be taken care of on the phone?"

"No," he barked. "If not in my office, then where? This can't be discussed on the telephone." After a pause, he snapped, "Where are you?"

"I'm at home," Marcel said, her own irritation beginning to show.

"Then I'll be there in ten minutes," he said and hung up.

Marcel stood there holding the phone in disbelief. "He's coming over," she said, and looked at her mother.

"Here? What does he want?" Roslin got up and immediately began straightening the two magazines on a small table near the fireplace. The house was immaculate, but Roslin apparently had an urge to find something to clean.

After hanging up with the General, Marcel called the shop to see if Carmen was still there. When she answered, Marcel asked her what Jordan had wanted when she'd called yesterday.

"She didn't say, but she didn't sound like herself either. More subdued than usual."

"Okay, thanks."

"Wait!" Carmen said before Marcel hung up again. "Cricket's still here."

In the next second, Cricket was on the phone. "Is your mother there by chance?"

Marcel rolled her eyes and held the phone out to her mother. "Here. It's for you."

General Wheatly was punctual, and Marcel didn't want to think about how or why he knew where she lived. Her address was no secret, but this was a man who was accustomed to being driven everywhere, having doors opened and calls placed for him. But here he was standing on her porch in his uniform, which Marcel imagined to be just one more attempt to intimidate her. Jordan had commented once that Big Boy even had his rank sewn on his pajamas, and seeing him now made Marcel remember that and smile.

"General Wheatly," she said as she opened the door wider for him. "Please come in. What brings you out on a day like this?" The thunder had gradually been moving closer, and flashes of lightning lit up the dark sky.

"I need a word with you in private," he said.

Marcel could hear her mother giggling on the phone in the other room, and she knew that after tending to the General, she'd have a little discussion with her about Cricket. *Giggling,* Marcel thought. *My mother's giggling, for crissakes!*

"We can talk in my study," she said and led the way down the hall. She offered him something to drink, but he declined.

Marcel was a bit relieved by that because she didn't want him there any longer than necessary. She closed the door and nodded toward one of the two chairs in the room near her desk.

"I'll get right to the point," he said. "I have a meeting with my lawyer in an hour." He sat down and for the first time Marcel noticed how angry he was. "My wife has informed me that she's been having . . . an *affair* with you."

He said the word *affair* as though he were coughing up a fur ball. Marcel initially thought he was joking, but as she zeroed in on his anger again, it was clear how serious he was.

"I'll be divorcing her and suing you for alienation of affection. In addition, I suggest you get ready to fork over every last cent the United States Army has paid you over the years." Under his breath she heard him mumble, "Dyke bitch." He snapped his head up and said, "I also plan to ensure you never see any of your retirement check!"

Marcel stared at him. Key words and phrases were bouncing around in her head . . . *affair, alienation of affection, divorce, dyke bitch*. She couldn't believe he had invited himself into her home only to accuse her of something so outrageous.

"You can't even deny it," he said in a vicious spew as he twitched in his chair.

"I don't even know where to begin," Marcel said. *"Jordan* told you this?" *Jordan called yesterday,* Marcel remembered suddenly. *And Carmen said she had sounded strange.*

"I've taken care of my wife. Now I'm taking care of you."

"Don't believe everything you hear, General."

"Why would she lie about you, but admit sleeping with a dyke?"

"I can't begin to explain her motives for anything."

"Stop it! Stop it right now!" he yelled.

"Excuse me? How dare you come into my home and talk to me this way! You can take your threats and put them —"

"You think these are threats? You're very wrong there, Colonel. These are promises!"

"Why," Marcel said, raising her voice to match his, "why would you *think* of taking something like this public? Alienation of affection. You'll not only be the laughing stock of San Antonio and Fort Sam Houston, but of the entire Armed Forces!"

"Scum like you in uniform for twenty years," he seethed. "You make me sick!"

"I'm admitting to nothing. You *have* nothing."

"You don't have to admit to anything. My wife already did that for you. I'll see you in court."

He got up and left, slamming the door on his way out of the study. Marcel could hear her mother's cheerful voice greeting him in the hallway before she came into Marcel's study with a raised eyebrow.

"I heard yelling," Roslin said. "What did he want?"

Marcel crossed her arms over her chest and leaned back against the corner of her desk. Her mind was racing as she attempted to process what had just happened.

"Marcel."

"I'm not ready to talk about it yet," Marcel said.

"No fair! That's my line!"

Shaking with anger, Marcel wondered why Jordan would lie about such a thing. Marcel rebuffing Jordan's advances had almost become a game for them. Amanda's face immediately popped into her head and she thought suddenly, *Two women in two days have lied about me.* Marcel felt sick.

"Hey," Roslin said gently. "What did he want? You're so pale. You're scaring me."

"He's a bit irrational right now, I think." She didn't have Jordan's phone number with her, then remembered that it was probably on Jordan's check from the desk purchase over the weekend.

"Why will he be seeing you in court? That much I heard."

Marcel left the study to get her briefcase where the weekend's receipts were. Roslin was right behind her, asking a string of questions only to receive a series of grunts from

Marcel. After finally locating her briefcase and rummaging through it in search of Jordan's check, she snatched it up and began dialing.

"You're ignoring me," Roslin said, "and you know how I hate that."

"What's good for the goose is good for the goose."

Roslin squinted at her with a puzzled expression.

"It's a lesbian expression," Marcel said. "No ganders. Two geese. Never mind."

"What in the world are you talking about?"

"Never mind. Never mind." When the Wheatlys' answering machine kicked in, Marcel felt anxious and on the verge of raw emotion. "Jordan," she said after the canned greeting finished. "If you're there answer the phone. It's Marcel. I need to talk to you."

She was relieved to hear someone pick up the phone. "Marcel."

"Jordan? Is that you?"

"Yes," came the low breathy whisper. "I'm so sorry." Jordan was crying and Marcel's anger and frustration diminished a bit. "I can't talk. He's given me an hour to get out."

"Did he hurt you?"

"He slapped me a few times, but I pushed him into it."

"Do you have a place to go?"

"I'm going to Heidi's house. She won't like it, but I'm going there anyway. I can't talk now."

"Wait!" Marcel said. "Isn't there somewhere else you can go? If he finds you at Captain Cooper's house, he'll make things impossible for her. For both of you."

In a near whisper Jordan said, "I've taken care of that already. I've sold you out, Marcel. I told him I was having an affair with you so he'd stop looking. You're out of the Army now. He can't hurt you."

Marcel's breathing changed, and her anger came back with such intensity that she began shaking. "You told him it was me," she said through clenched teeth. For some reason, hearing Jordan say it was a thousand times worse than hearing the General say it.

"I had to. He caught me in a lie I couldn't talk my way out of." Jordan had stopped crying now and was beginning to sound more like her usual spunky self. "And I figured he couldn't do anything to you now that you're retired. He wanted a name and —"

"I've spent years," Marcel said in a low, eerie voice. "Years being selective about who I spend my time with. Years nurturing my reputation just so I could finally do what I love doing. And here you are. You come along and accuse me of something like this and throw it all away. Cheapening my life for what? To save your girlfriend's career?"

"I have to go, Marcel."

"Jordan, so help me . . ." Marcel was too angry to even finish her sentence. She hung up the phone and closed her eyes, hoping that her fury would pass before she did something dangerously irrational.

"Start talking," Roslin said as she led Marcel to the sofa. "Tell me everything."

Chapter Fourteen

Marcel had gotten forty-five minutes worth of sleep and finally just got out of bed at five o'clock the next morning to begin her day. Her mother's concern and willingness to find a solution to what she referred to as "the Wheatly problem" had kept them up into the wee hours of the morning. At one point Roslin was ready to call one of her gambling friends from New York and have him arrange to have "a word" with the General.

"I'm sure Mr. Battaglia can have his boys here in no time," Roslin said over her third glass of wine. "They can make cement combat boots in the General's size, I'm sure."

"And where would they throw him?" Marcel asked. "The San Antonio river is barely deep enough to float a canoe."

Roslin cut loose with a wine-induced cackle. "Okay, okay, okay. So here's what we do. Instead of the cement boots, I'll see if they can make a special cement helmet for him and we'll throw him in the river headfirst. How's that?"

Marcel was never quite sure how many, if any, of her mother's gambling acquaintances were unsavory characters. She did know, however, that her mother had friends all over the world—-some in high places. And if the General were to come up missing at some point, Marcel would have no trouble asking her mother where the authorities needed to look for him.

"How much sleep did you get?" Carmen asked as soon as Marcel arrived at the Antique Villa.

"An hour. Does it show?"

"Far be it from me to tell you that you look like hell. A trip to the doctor should be agenda material, I think."

"What I need," Marcel said tiredly, "is to get my life in order."

"You've had that before and it didn't work. You still couldn't sleep." Carmen pulled up a chair and insisted that Marcel sit down. She then went to the tiny kitchen area in the back and returned with a steaming cup of herbal tea. "Drink this," Carmen said. "It'll relax you."

"Is this more of that kelp concoction you tried to give me once?"

"No. This is worse, but drink it anyway."

As Marcel sat and held her cup, Carmen rubbed her shoulders with slow, soothing movements.

"Your mother told me how upset Cricket still is with you," Carmen said.

Marcel closed her eyes and felt limp like a noodle. "When did you talk to her? She was asleep when I left this morning."

"Yesterday, after Cricket left here."

Carmen's fingers moved from Marcel's shoulders to her neck, and Marcel was close to a dreamlike state when Carmen spoke again.

"You're not drinking."

Marcel sighed and took a sip of the hot tea. "This stuff stinks. What is it?"

"Just drink. It'll help relax you."

"I'm already relaxed."

Carmen gently rubbed both sides of her neck, her ears, and her temples. "There is something else," Carmen said. "I can feel it. Tell me what you're thinking right now."

"I'm thinking," Marcel said dreamily as she took another sip from the mug, "that we'd be rich if you'd find a way to bottle a massage." She could hear Carmen's soft chuckle as though she were far away.

"Drink," Carmen said again, and Marcel took another sip. "We have a bed in there for you if you get sleepy."

Marcel smiled. "Thanks. Maybe later. By the way. Guess what happened to me last night? I had a visit from General Wheatly." She went on to explain her conversation with him.

"So you are sleeping with Jordan," Carmen said. Her fingers stopped massaging and rested on Marcel's shoulders.

"Of course not," Marcel said. "That's just what Jordan told him." She turned her head and looked up at Carmen, who seemed to be scrutinizing her in return. "I can't believe you asked me that."

"Hey, these are strange times. You're sleeping with Amanda, and now Cricket's kissing your mother. Nothing would surprise me, I guess." She started massaging Marcel's neck again.

"I was only with Amanda once."

"That's not what Cricket says. Drink some more tea."

"Cricket can go piss up a rope," Marcel mumbled. "I can't believe all these rumors that are flying around. Oh, and I didn't even tell you about the best part of the General's visit last night. He plans to sue me for alienation of affection."

The hands stopped massaging again. "Is he serious?"

"He sounded serious."

Carmen's laughter echoed throughout the entire showroom. "This is *great!* Every wire service in the country will pick it up. You can't beat publicity like that." Her fingers began moving again with renewed vigor. "This will be so good for business. We won't be able to keep up!"

Marcel looked at her in amazement. "He's threatening to drag my name through the mud and all you can think about is how good it'll be for business?"

"They'll come flocking to see you. Tabloids, newspapers, CNN, *The Army Times!* And we'll only grant them interviews if they buy something."

Marcel groaned when she realized that Carmen was teasing her.

"You really never slept with Jordan?"

"No, I never slept with Jordan. Never wanted to and never plan to. She's lying to protect her girlfriend."

"And who's her girlfriend?" Carmen prompted.

"Depends on which day of the week it is, I think."

By early afternoon Marcel was winding down, and she was relieved to know that she'd be able to sleep that night. She had felt less anxious and a tad bit mellow after finishing the tea Carmen had made for her. Off and on during the day, Carmen would pop in from her work area to remind her that there was a bed in Marcel's office if she got sleepy.

"I can handle things here," Carmen said. She had a paint smudge on her cheek and what appeared to be sawdust in her hair.

"What have you been doing back there?" Marcel asked.

"Killing more spiders mostly."

The door dinged, announcing the arrival of another customer.

"Hello," Naomi said. "I got your call about finding a table I might be interested in."

"I have it in the back," Carmen said.

Marcel had no idea what they were talking about. "Carmen called you," she said after a moment.

"Yes," Naomi said. "This morning, in fact." Naomi put her elbows on the counter and smiled engagingly as she leaned forward. Her dark curls framed an interesting, oval face. She was attractive, with dark brown eyes and an endearing crooked smile. Marcel was glad to see her and was flattered by Naomi's obvious interest in her.

"So," Naomi said. "Will you have dinner with me tonight? I plan to keep asking, so you might as well say yes now and get it over with."

Marcel liked Naomi's persistence and found it refreshing, but she was a bit concerned about getting involved with someone that Cricket had an eye on. Marcel's relationship with Cricket didn't need another damaging blow so soon after the Amanda incident.

"Dinner," Naomi said again. "Just two people having dinner. You have to eat anyway, so why not do it with me?"

Carmen came in from the workshop carrying the small table. "Is this what you were looking for?" She set it down and then stood back to admire it.

"Perfect," Naomi said with a smile.

Carmen nodded and returned to her work area in the back of the shop. Naomi was obviously pleased with the find and wrote a check for her purchase.

"Dinner," she said again as she handed the check over. Her smile was shy, and Marcel saw something in her eyes that she hadn't noticed before. Marcel sensed a reining-in of something new, something resembling desire and eagerness, as though Naomi wanted to say more and do more but thought it wiser not to. This "something" that Marcel saw touched her in a way she had never experienced before. It went beyond flattery and hovered near a stronger, deeper feeling. Naomi's attention and easygoing manner struck a chord in Marcel, and she allowed herself to accept it a bit more easily. Something else also came to her as Naomi slid her driver's license across the counter. Marcel took the check and handed the license back to her without looking at it, but remembered what Carmen had said about Naomi after the grand opening. *The other two want to bed you. This one wants to know you.*

Marcel finished the transaction and said, "Dinner at seven sound okay?"

Trying to appear cool even though her eyes were dancing, Naomi said, "Seven's fine. I'll meet you somewhere. What sounds good?"

"Let's keep it simple," Marcel said, and then suggested a coffee shop just down the street. She offered to help Naomi get the table in her car.

Marcel held the door open and then suggested they try getting it in the backseat. After rearranging a few things, the table was safely in place.

"Seven," Naomi said as she dropped her car keys in the parking lot for the second time.

"Seven," Marcel repeated. She waved and then went back inside only to find Carmen behind the counter shaking her head.

"The General is suing you because you're sleeping with his wife. Your best friend isn't talking to you because you slept with her girlfriend. And now I overhear you making a date with —"

"I never slept with the General's wife," Marcel reminded her pointedly. "Why do you keep forgetting that?"

"It's just a technicality. You know what? Maybe you *should* have slept with her since we all think you did anyway."

"I've got the truth on my side."

"Whoop-de-do."

~ ~ ~ ~ ~

Naomi was waiting in the restaurant's parking lot when

Marcel arrived. Marcel was tired and knew better than to start thinking about how quickly she would be able to fall asleep when she got home. Anticipating sleep was the second fastest way she knew of to keep her awake, with number one on the list still being sex. But as far as the sex thing went, Marcel always kept in mind that if she had to be awake anyway, she might as well be happy while she was doing it.

"The table fits perfectly next to my sofa at home," Naomi said. "I appreciate your finding it for me."

"Not a problem. That's a big part of what I do now."

They located a table in the restaurant, scanned the menus, and gave their orders to the waitress. Marcel settled into the booth comfortably and couldn't believe how relaxed and good she felt.

"How was your day?" Naomi asked. Her hands were folded on the table, and Marcel noticed the sparkle in her dark brown eyes.

"My day was busy. How was yours?"

"The cars parked on both sides of me at school today had their hubcaps stolen. At first I felt guilty because mine had been spared, but then I saw how silly that was."

"A nice stroke of luck."

Naomi nodded. "When something good happens to me, I have trouble accepting it sometimes. But I think things happen for a reason." She took a sip of her water. "Do you believe in destiny?"

"I'm a romantic," Marcel said. "I believe in everything." She found herself being unexpectedly entertained as dinner progressed. The conversation never once turned serious, and there was no further indication that Naomi was nervous about being with her. Marcel enjoyed her company and liked Naomi's insight and her ability to laugh at herself.

Marcel noticed that the more time they spent together, the better she liked it. At one point during dinner, she again admitted to herself that she was attracted to Naomi, and only briefly wondered how that could have happened so quickly since less than a week ago she had thought she was in love with Amanda. *It's Naomi's honesty,* she thought. *Everything about her is right there in her eyes. And she's funny. She makes me laugh. I need more of that in my life right now.*

In the parking lot after dinner, they made plans to do it again on Thursday night. Marcel liked thinking of it as a date and pushed all thought of Naomi's being Cricket's latest obsession out of her head. She got in her car and drove home yawning, which delighted her. Sleep would come easily that night and would help recharge her batteries for the week.

When she got home, she heard her mother talking to someone in the living room. Marcel peeked around the corner and saw that Roslin was on the phone. They waved, and Roslin covered the receiver to let her know that she was talking to Cricket. Marcel pantomimed a yawn and pointed toward the stairs.

"And tell Cricket that I had a date tonight with one of her girlfriends," Marcel said loudly enough for Cricket to hear on the other end of the phone.

Roslin laughed. "Cricket heard you and is being quite colorful right now, dear."

Marcel woke up at seven the next morning and felt groggy. Knowing that Carmen would be at the shop to take care of things made moving quickly less of an emergency.

Roslin was already up and dressed, and she handed her a steaming cup of decaf as soon as she shuffled into the kitchen.

"I've taken the liberty of speaking to a lawyer for you," Roslin said. "About the General Wheatly thing."

"Oh," Marcel said. Her voice was still laced with sleep.

"And once the lawyer stopped laughing, she said that the General would be crazy to do it, but we can't stop him."

"Didn't we know that already?"

"We did, but now it's official. His trying to have your

retirement benefits revoked is ridiculous," Roslin said. "I'm not sure he's playing with a full deck, as we say in my profession." She handed Marcel two slices of cinnamon toast. "You finally got some sleep, baby?"

"Yes. Finally."

"Can I handle the General problem for you?" Roslin asked sweetly.

Marcel smiled and answered just as sweetly, "You can, as long as he doesn't end up with cement on any part of his body."

Chapter Fifteen

Marcel wasn't quite sure what to expect the next time she met Amanda, but the anger she felt when she saw her wasn't a surprise. Marcel was at an office supply store getting supplies for the shop when she literally ran into her near a fax-machine display. Rolls of cash register tape and a package of sales-receipt books went in several directions as she and Amanda stared at each other.

"Hi," Amanda finally said while handing over a box of price tags that had landed on her foot.

"I've got it. Thanks."

Amanda let her hands fall to her sides. "I'm sorry I never got back to you. Things have been —"

"Don't give me another thought," Marcel said quietly. She

turned and went to stand in line at the checkout counter and managed to reel in her anger. It was the lying that she had hated the most — not so much that Amanda and Cricket were still together, or that Amanda had never called her after that night. Marcel firmly believed that Amanda had never intended to tell Cricket that they had slept together, and that hurt. She was also wondering if maybe the only reason Amanda had slept with her at all was in order to get back at Cricket for being interested in Naomi. That scenario was beginning to look more like the truth than anything else, and it made Marcel feel cheap and used.

Once she was finished in line, Marcel collected her purchases and went outside into the April afternoon heat only to find Amanda waiting for her at the car.

"Let me at least try to explain," Amanda said. Marcel ignored her and unlocked her car door. "Please."

"Explain to me why you lied about wanting to tell Cricket about us," Marcel said simply. Horrified at being close to tears, she tossed the bag of supplies in her front seat and said, "On second thought, it doesn't matter." She tried to get in her car, but Amanda held on to the door and wouldn't let her open it all the way.

"Please, Marcel. Don't do this. Let me explain."

"I said it doesn't matter."

"Things changed once I saw Cricket again."

Marcel glared at her and said, "Let go of the door."

"I couldn't do it. I —"

"Let go of the door."

Amanda removed her hand from the door, but didn't get out of the way. "I haven't handled this very well."

"A gross understatement."

"I never meant to hurt you."

"As I said before, don't give me another thought. I do have a question, though. Why does Cricket think I called you at the club that night? Why does she think that?"

Amanda's eyes widened, and she immediately turned pale.

Marcel held the look and showed no mercy in her contempt. Amanda backpedaled away from the car. Marcel got in her car and drove away. How she ever thought she could have been in love with that woman was a mystery.

"I think we have the General's attention," Roslin said later that evening as she steadily packed her suitcase. Marcel was stretched out on the end of Roslin's bed with her head propped up. She had been watching her mother pack for business trips ever since she was a kid. Some of their best talks had taken place as toiletries were put into resealable plastic bags.

"I made a little call to one of my senator friends," Roslin said. "We've been gambling associates for years, and he owes me more favors than he cares to remember. Anyway, it looks like the General is about to be reassigned."

"He's not due to leave here for another year yet," Marcel said skeptically.

"Not now! Special assignment. He'll be gone in two weeks."

Marcel sat up. "Are they promoting him? Is he getting another star out of this?"

"Special assignment. No more stars." With a wink she added, "I took care of that, too." Roslin carefully folded a nightgown and placed it in the suitcase. "He'll forget all about this as soon as he's rubbing elbows at the Pentagon again."

Marcel didn't trust her mother's "senator friend" or anyone else for that matter. She had an appointment with a lawyer the next day and wanted a better idea about what to expect with all of this lawsuit business. Her lawyer's suggestion about countersuing the Wheatlys for both libel and slander was high on her list of priorities. "We'll countersue for both," the lawyer at said. "If we lose on one, we might win on the other."

"And if this little transfer thing doesn't work," Roslin said, "then I'll have to find those pictures I have of him in Tijuana." She neatly folded an elegant slip and tucked it in the suitcase. "But I hate having to resort to that. It's so . . . so . . . low and despicable."

"What pictures? Are you talking about pictures of the Senator or pictures of the General?"

"The Senator gave me pictures of the General." Roslin glanced around the room. "But I don't remember where I put them."

Marcel sat up a little straighter on the bed and cautiously watched her mother. A chill raced down her arms as she realized that things may not be quite as they seemed. "Please tell me you're kidding about all of this."

"Do I sound like I'm kidding?"

"Okay," Marcel said as she firmly planted her feet on the floor. "Tell me exactly what you've done so far. And start from the moment the General left this house the other night."

As Roslin talked and explained each move that had been made, anxiety started building in Marcel's chest. According to Roslin, a gambling acquaintance from New York had sent a few of his "boys" to San Antonio to have a word with the General. In the meantime, the Senator had put both of the Wheatlys under twenty-four-hour surveillance. Roslin's New York friend and the Senator were operating separately and didn't know what the other was doing, but Roslin assured Marcel that both parties only had her best interest in mind.

"Jordan is shacking up with Heidi Cooper, in case you weren't aware of who the other woman was," Roslin informed her smugly.

"I knew that already," Marcel said. Her head began to swim with all this information. She quickly collected her thoughts and said, "I want your friend from New York to have his . . . his *boys* go back home. And I want you to tell the Senator to drop the surveillance on the Wheatlys."

144

"But we're just getting started!"

"This has gotten totally out of control. Totally."

"He's playing dirty so —"

"But that's not the way I do things." Marcel looked at her mother as if she were seeing a stranger. "And you should know that already."

Silk panties were folded with more emphasis than before and then were stuffed in the suitcase as if being punished. "How I raised such a little patriot I'll never know. Let me handle this, Marcel."

"It's my problem. I'll take care of it." Marcel could tell by the way her mother continued folding her clothes with exaggerated motions that she was mad and not listening to her. "I mean it," Marcel warned.

"I've gone to a lot of trouble. You're putting me in an awkward position here."

Marcel knew she didn't have to say anything else. She left her mother alone to finish packing for her trip, and she could trust that the appropriate phone calls would be made later.

At nine-thirty while working in her study, Marcel heard her mother answer the doorbell. The sound of a cheerful but muffled female voice didn't give away who the visitor was, but when Roslin didn't knock on Marcel's door, it was evident that the visitor wasn't there to see her.

Marcel had some bookkeeping to do and a bank deposit for the week's receipts to prepare for the next day. She also had the newspaper handy so that she could search for estate sales going on that week. Business was excellent, and the Antique Villa was showing a sizable profit already. Keeping up with the steady demand for fresh inventory was Marcel's biggest job at the moment.

Needing something to drink a while later, Marcel headed

toward the kitchen. She heard what she thought sounded like groaning coming from the living room, and she stopped to peek around the corner. A bare leg was draped over the top of the sofa; the rose tattoo near the bare ankle belonged to her mother, and Cricket's green backpack was on the floor nearby.

Marcel was in shock as she stared at the tattoo, but her shock was immediately replaced by anger. The sight of her mother having sex at all was unthinkable. Not to mention *lesbian* sex!

Marcel edged back down the hallway and returned to her office. She closed the door quietly and leaned against it, stunned. *Maybe that wasn't my mother's leg I just saw,* she thought, grasping for a reasonable explanation, but she knew better. She would know that tattoo anywhere.

Two hours later, still "trapped" in her study, Marcel glanced at her watch and wondered how long she would have to stay there. She couldn't believe how careless her mother had been . . . how insensitive and foolish their actions were. Had her mother forgotten that Marcel was still in the house? Having spent the last twenty-four years of her life in a closeted environment where the smallest indiscretion could have ruined her career or thrown suspicion her way, Marcel had very low tolerance for such behavior. She kept going over things in her head. *Is it because my mother is having lesbian sex?* she wondered. *Is it because she's out there going at it on the sofa? Or because it's Cricket, my best friend. Cricket, the lesbian social butterfly?*

Marcel was not at all happy with this new development. Cricket was the last person in the world whom she wanted her mother involved with! *So is that it?* she wondered suddenly. *If it were someone other than Cricket out there making love to my mother, would that be better?* Marcel visibly cringed at just *thinking* about the phrase *making love to my mother!*

"I can't believe my mother is doing this," Marcel mumbled. *Why isn't she in her room? Did she want me to find them?*

Marcel tapped her pencil on the tablet as she looked at her watch again. She had read every word in the newspaper already and had posted all the daily sales for the week to the computer. She had even called Carmen at home to tell her how successful the business had been lately.

Trying to stay calm and keep busy, she made it a point not to think too much. A while later as she made a list of addresses for the estate sales she intended to check out during the week, Marcel heard rustling and giggling in the hallway. Several minutes later, there was a light knock on her door, and her mother came in looking animated and disheveled. Roslin's eyes sparkled and her cheeks were flushed. Marcel thought she was absolutely radiant.

Leaning against the door, her hand still touching the knob as she looked at Marcel, Roslin said, "You never told me. Or if you did I never heard you."

Marcel glared at her, still too shocked to think clearly. "I never told you what?" she asked shortly.

Roslin closed her eyes and took a deep breath. "How good it is. How incredible it can be!"

Marcel couldn't believe they were having this conversation. "I heard you two out there. I saw you."

Roslin's smile and euphoria slowly disappeared. "Oh."

"Oh?" Marcel repeated. "That's all you have to say?"

"You're upset."

"Of *course* I'm upset! I walked in on my mother having sex. How would *you* feel?"

Roslin sat down in one of the chairs near Marcel's desk. "I see what you mean. I'm sorry, baby."

"Five bedrooms in this house and where do I find you?"

Marcel's anger and shock were so tightly wound together that she still couldn't think clearly. "And with Cricket," she said. "*Cricket*! Of all people!"

Roslin cocked her head and looked at her slowly. "Are you upset because it was Cricket?"

Marcel was suddenly forced to stop and consider the question. "That's only part of it."

"Talk to me. What's going on in that head of yours?"

Their voices were back to normal again, and Marcel no longer had the urge to pace or express herself at a high volume.

"Three things," Marcel said simply. "The first one being that my mother has sex at all," she admitted with a series of nods and shrugs. This made Roslin laugh.

"Okay," Roslin said. "I'll give you that one. I was always convinced that my parents only had sex once, so I understand completely. What else?"

"It was just a shock. You and Cricket. You know how she is."

"This has nothing to do with any of that," Roslin said. "All I know is that I like her and I like this new thing I've discovered with her."

Marcel noticed that her mother at least had the decency to be embarrassed.

Roslin continued. "And I'm sorry that I showed bad judgment by carrying on so in our living room. At the time it was happening, I honestly forgot that you were here."

Marcel nodded and accepted the apology, but she was still at a loss as to how best to deal with her feelings about everything.

"I'm canceling my flight tomorrow," Roslin said. "I can't go anywhere like this."

Marcel began tapping her pencil against the tablet again, and for the first time since all of this had happened, she got worried. Nothing except bad weather ever affected her mother's work schedule. Business was business, and a flight cancellation right now was indeed serious.

"So tell me what's happening with you," Marcel said. "How are you feeling about everything?"

Roslin shook her head. "You mean about what happened with Cricket?"

Marcel nodded.

"I'm . . . I'm excited and giddy. Confused, surprised, happy, and afraid. All of the above."

Marcel asked her what she was afraid of.

"How good I feel. How happy I am."

Cricket, Marcel thought. *My mother's involved with Cricket, for crissakes!* Cricket had the attention span of a gnat when it came to relationships.

"Maybe you shouldn't cancel your trip," Marcel suggested. "Getting away right now might be good for you."

"I can't work like this. I need to be focused."

Marcel nodded and had to agree that losing fifty thousand dollars or so due to poor concentration was an expensive way to get one's perspective back. "So what's happening with you two now? Are you dating? Exploring? Playing? What?" She still couldn't believe they were having this conversation.

Roslin shrugged. "I'm exploring. She's playing." As if hearing herself for the first time, Roslin stopped and seemed to come to her senses a little. "You're right. Maybe I shouldn't cancel my flight tomorrow. I need to get back to what I know."

"Sleep on it. Everything might be clearer in the morning."

Marcel watched as her mother struggled with having to decide what to do. Finally Roslin gave up and chose to go to bed.

"Will you be able to sleep tonight?" she asked as she kissed Marcel on top of the head.

"The usual."

"Then I'll see you in the morning. And I'm sorry you had to see all of that earlier. I'll be more discreet in the future."

149

The future, Marcel thought with a groan. *So there will be more of this in the future?*

As the night dragged on, Marcel wondered briefly if she would ever get sleepy again. She stayed busy researching furniture pieces on the computer and checked out a few Web sites she'd been hearing about. The more tired she became, the less patience she had. Several times she had tried to call Cricket, but the line was constantly busy. Marcel needed a change and wanted to clear the air and her mind a bit. She found her keys and drove to Cricket's house to get a few answers, but only with the understanding that she would return home without stopping if Amanda's car was there.

"Do you know what time it is?" Cricket said when she opened her door. Cricket's shorts and T-shirt told Marcel that she hadn't been to bed yet either, and Cricket had to be at work in a few hours.

"You've ruined my life," Cricket informed her dramatically. She went over to the phone and picked up the dangling receiver. "I have to go. I'll call you tomorrow. Yes, I know it's tomorrow already. I can't talk now. Good-bye." Storming to the kitchen, she poured herself some wine. Marcel followed her and was willing to wait until Cricket calmed down a little before trying to say anything.

"Amanda is on my case wanting an answer," Cricket said, "and Naomi won't even talk to me now. What am I supposed to do? I work with her. It's very awkward."

"You could start by dating one person at a time like most normal people."

Cricket set her wineglass down on the kitchen counter and turned around. "Amanda wants us to get back together and forget about what's happened. I'm supposed to pretend that she never slept with you, and then she'll pretend that I never chased after Naomi. It's like we're even or something." Her voice had finally lost its projecting ability. "And now I'm wondering if Amanda didn't sleep with you just to make me jealous."

Bingo, Marcel thought.

"And Naomi is totally enthralled with you, which pisses me off too," Cricket continued. "Who the hell do you think you are? Isn't anything sacred to you?"

Marcel took a deep breath and glared at her. "At least I never slept with your mother."

"Don't even start with me!"

"I'm here to do a lot more than that, kiddo."

"It's not what you think," Cricket said. She picked up her wineglass again and took a healthy gulp. "It's not what you think," she repeated more calmly. "I'm in love with her, Marcel. Ever since I was a kid I've been in love with her."

Marcel couldn't deny that there was some truth in that statement. "Tell me what happened the day you kissed her."

Cricket shook her head. "That whole day was very strange. I had this dream about her," she said quietly. "A very vivid, hot dream. We were making love, and in my dream I kept thinking that I should wake up, but I didn't. It was so wonderful and real. I've never had a dream like that before.

"So the next morning and all that day I couldn't think about anything else. And the *really* weird thing was that in the dream your mother never discouraged any of my advances. So I kept thinking about that and couldn't get it out of my head. All day long. Over and over. I couldn't concentrate at work. I was sitting through green lights in traffic. It got so bad that I went to see her that next afternoon." Cricket set her glass down again.

"So I get to your house and your mother and I are in the living room and we're talking about you and your retirement and you and Amanda, and she's being very nice to me like she always is. I wasn't getting any vibes from her, you know? At least not the vibes I was looking for anyway. Then I got scared." Cricket slowly rubbed her arms as if she were cold.

"I got scared because I was afraid the dream was just that — just a silly dream. So I stalled a little in hopes that something would happen — a sign or something. *Something!* But nothing happened. Then it was time for me to go. She walks me to the front door and I'm still waiting for something to happen, and then I realize that it's all up to me. *I'm* the one who has to get things going. *I'm* the one who has to make something happen." Cricket smiled a little at the memory.

"So I stopped thinking so much and on impulse I leaned over and kissed her." Cricket turned her head and looked at Marcel. "And she opened her mouth." Cricket closed her eyes and visibly trembled at what was for her a very powerful memory. "And when her tongue touched mine, I thought I would faint, Marcel. I thought I would fucking faint."

Marcel chuckled, but had no choice but to believe her. Cricket's reaction was too real to have been made up.

"Then I ran out the door and jumped in my car and went directly to see you. I don't remember driving there or parking my car." Cricket cleared her throat and then leaned her head back and closed her eyes. "I'm in love with her. I've always been in love with her."

"Then what's going on with Amanda? And why are you still playing footsie with Naomi?"

"It's over with Amanda. I just haven't told her yet." She moved her shoulders and then rubbed the back of her neck. "That was Amanda on the phone. She still wants me to move in with her, and I don't know how to tell her that I can't." She drained her wineglass and filled it with water from the tap. "But I'm thoroughly pissed at you for sleeping with her. Amanda was still mine when you did that. Some friend you are. And not to mention the way you've snatched Naomi right out from under me, so to speak. I liked her too for a while there, but did that make a difference to you?"

"When did you start taking up this bad habit of juggling all these women at one time?"

"I'm in the process of changing my ways."

"Sure you are. My mother's at home thinking you're the best thing since Post Toasties and you're here on the phone negotiating living arrangements with Amanda." Marcel looked at her. She wanted no doubt or misunderstanding between them. "Until you get it more together, stay away from my mother."

Cricket's doorbell rang, and they both jumped at the same time before glancing at their watches. It was two-thirty in the morning! Marcel was ready to leave; she had made her point and felt certain that she had given Cricket a few things to think about already.

Marcel found her keys in her pocket and waited for Cricket to answer the door. As Marcel saw her mother standing there in the dim light of the porch, she was too surprised to say anything. But the moment Cricket opened her arms and kissed Roslin, that was all it took for Marcel to see everything differently. In her mind Cricket was no longer just her best friend. Cricket Lomax had become her mother's lover.

Chapter Sixteen

Thursday morning Marcel returned to the shop after meeting with her lawyer again. It was a relief to hear that General Wheatly hadn't dropped his lawsuit yet. That meant the visitors from New York were gone and nothing dreadful had happened to anyone. But Marcel was fuming at the General's misguided revenge. She had given her lawyer permission to countersue the Wheatlys for libel and slander if the General continued with his threat to sue her for alienation of affection. As Marcel tried to explain all of this to Carmen later that morning, Marcel still failed to see any humor in the situation.

"Come on," Carmen chided. "Lighten up."

"It's all lies!" Marcel said in exasperation. "Why should I put up with this? Why should I let him do this to me when what he's accusing me of isn't true?"

"Yeah, I know. You're right. Maybe we need to find out where Jordan is staying and take a few snapshots of her in action."

"You sound like my mother."

"Your mother makes sense sometimes." Carmen leaned against the counter and shrugged. "So what's the deal?" she asked. "Are you going back in the closet until this thing blows over?"

Marcel raised an eyebrow at the question.

"Because if you are," Carmen continued, "you need to take that rainbow sticker off your car."

Her laughter didn't do much to put Marcel in a better mood. "I'm glad you find this so amusing," Marcel said. "My life's in the toilet, and all you can do is laugh."

"I'll say it again. You should let your mother handle this. She's got an interesting way with people. General Wheatly wouldn't know what hit him."

"And that's exactly what I'm afraid of."

Hours later the door to the shop dinged open and Marcel looked up and smiled when she saw Naomi. Seeing her again made Marcel feel warm inside. Once again she tried to figure out what she found so attractive about her, and the word *charisma* popped in her head once more. It was nothing really tangible, but very effective just the same.

Naomi was wearing black slacks and a white shirt. A black bolo tie set off the outfit perfectly and was a nice complement to her dark curly hair. Being one of those women who could make flannel look feminine, Naomi was elegant and unpretentious, a combination that Marcel found quite sexy.

"I was wondering if you were free for lunch," Naomi said. "I have to be back at work in a little over an hour, but I thought I'd give it a shot."

Marcel glanced at her watch. She hadn't realized how late it was already. She told Carmen where she was going and followed Naomi to the coffee shop down the street. Once they were seated, Naomi said, "I thought I'd have better luck if I just appeared instead of trying to talk you into it on the phone."

"You think it's that difficult to get me somewhere?"

With an impish grin, Naomi rearranged her silverware on the napkin. "You're kidding, right?"

The waitress came and took their orders. Marcel studied Naomi more closely and was drawn to her persistence as well as to the hint of shyness she saw.

"Getting your attention has been one of life's biggest challenges for me," Naomi said. "You're always so busy, and then if by chance I'm in a position to talk to you, we're usually surrounded by other people."

Marcel laced her fingers together on the table and met Naomi's sparkling eyes. "You have my complete attention now."

Naomi grinned and held the look. "Great. And here I am at a total loss for words."

They laughed for a moment, and Marcel realized how relaxed she felt.

"Will you have dinner with me tonight?" Naomi asked. "I've got a rack of lamb waiting for a chance to show off my cooking skills."

"Two meals in a row together?"

"Okay, then tomorrow night."

"I'm teasing you," Marcel said, delighted by the invitation. "Tonight is fine. Unless you've changed your mind already."

"Not a chance."

Lunch went by quickly. When Marcel returned to the shop, Carmen, who was with a customer, managed to give her a questioning look across the room. After they helped load a table into the back of a pickup, Carmen let her know that Amanda had called. Marcel dropped Amanda's message in the trash can without even reading it.

"Okay. What's going on now? Amanda, Naomi, Jordan. Is that everyone? I can't keep the names straight anymore. Oh yes. And Heidi Cooper, but I haven't seen her around here much lately."

"Do you intentionally add Jordan's name to that list just to piss me off, or is it an oversight?"

"It's an oversight," Carmen said sheepishly. "I see that lunch with Naomi made you cranky."

"Not at all. I've got you to thank for that."

After work Marcel went home and got ready for her dinner date with Naomi. Roslin wasn't home and hadn't left any indication that she'd been there at all since she had gone to Cricket's house the night before. Marcel was still having a little trouble imagining those two together, but the kiss in Cricket's doorway that she had witnessed the night before had been anything but platonic. As Marcel had let herself out of Cricket's house last night, she'd gotten a healthy glimpse of where things were headed for them and had resigned herself to the fact that her mother was having a lesbian affair with a woman her daughter's age.

She decided to check out her mother's recently acquired wine cellar in the hope of finding something suitable for the evening at Naomi's. Marcel noticed that her mother had marked her favorite wines with notes to remind her which ones to drink first. Her mother had won the collection from a local car dealer after refusing to take another new car from him at the end of a poker game. His reluctance to part with his wine collection, however, made Roslin want it even that much more.

There were times when Roslin and her friends played for "things" such as art, uncirculated coins, vacation homes, land, or buildings instead of money. With the proper paperwork passed back and forth, depending on one's luck at the table, transactions were settled at the end of each evening. There were several items Roslin would never gamble with, and others that she had no problem losing.

Marcel switched the light on in the wine cellar and curled her nose at the mustiness in the small room. Most wine bottles had a yellow Post-it attached, and Marcel enjoyed reading what her mother had written — "A tad sweet, my favorite!" "Good with anything!" "So-so." "Probably good with fish."

Marcel picked up another bottle with a note that said, "Gave me a hangover! Serve only to someone I don't like!" Marcel chuckled and put that bottle back. She didn't find anything that directly addressed lamb, so she selected her mother's favorite.

Just before leaving, Marcel found the address that Naomi had written down for her; she was vaguely familiar with the area. Feeling a bit carefree and adventurous, she drove the Miata with the top down. Having hair that took no more than a few cleverly placed tosses to get it back into shape, Marcel made it a point not to worry or to think about anything. If the General sued her, then so be it. If her business collapsed, then it wasn't meant to be. If her mother and Cricket became devoted lovers, then why should she begrudge them their happiness? Marcel felt relaxed and unaffected. The four hours of sleep she'd gotten the night before would probably be the most she'd get for several days to come, and she still felt rested and rejuvenated because of it.

As she sped down the busy streets of San Antonio, Marcel kept remembering Naomi's laughter and that shock of dark curly hair. She had gotten the impression on several occasions that Naomi was a little shy and maybe a bit intimidated by her, but Marcel also saw the effort Naomi was making to overcome that. It was nice being with someone whose only agenda was finding ways to ask her out. Being pursued by someone she was attracted to was very nice and a different experience than what she was accustomed to.

She recognized Naomi's car in the driveway and parked behind it. After running her fingers through her hair, Marcel got the bottle of wine and wasn't a bit surprised by how much she was looking forward to this.

"Any trouble finding me?" Naomi asked when she answered the door.

Marcel handed the wine to her. "I found the place right away. Thanks." She took a deep breath and almost swooned. "It smells so-o-o good in here." She hadn't realized how hungry she was.

"Dinner should be ready in about fifteen minutes." Naomi led the way to the living room where an Enya CD was playing softly on the stereo. "Can I get you something to drink? I have a nice assortment of decaffeinated beverages and some decaf coffee I can put on. Or there's always wine." Naomi smiled and added, "Is it just me, or do I sound like a flight attendant?"

"It's just you," Marcel informed her with a laugh. *She remembered the caffeine thing,* Marcel thought. As Marcel processed that, she studied Naomi and liked what she saw. White cotton shorts, white sandals, and a gray V-neck pullover. There was kindness in her eyes, and a sense of longing that Marcel felt drawn to. *I've seen that look before,* she thought. *And I liked it then, too.*

"So what will it be?" Naomi asked. "Wine? Or something unleaded? I have caffeine-free drinks that are diet or —"

"I'll take a soft drink that doesn't have caffeine. It doesn't matter what kind." She laughed. "My mother calls any caffeine-free diet drink a *Why Bother?* She complains about them, but then that's all she keeps in the house."

"One *Why Bother?* coming up."

Naomi went to the kitchen with the wine bottle and

returned with two glasses of unleaded Diet Coke. "Your mother is a delightful woman, and she's very proud of you."

Marcel nodded. "I'm proud of her too."

"I understand she's a gambler. That alone makes her incredibly interesting. What does your father do?"

"My father died when I was young. He was a racecar driver. Very good at it. A popular figure in his country many years ago." Marcel set her drink down on a coaster on the coffee table as she remembered the stories her mother used to tell her about him. She still knew him through a child's eyes and often wondered what kind of man he had really been.

"You said 'in his country.' He wasn't an American?"

"He was French. I still have relatives in Paris."

"Hmm. Do you keep in touch with them?"

"My mother and I go back every two or three years to visit. We were last there in November. When I was a kid, I'd spend part of my summer there with my grandparents and my cousins. They visit us here sometimes too. My grandfather loves this one dude ranch in the Hill Country." Marcel laughed at the memory. "He likes being a cowboy in Texas."

After a moment, Naomi announced that dinner was ready. Marcel followed her to the kitchen and helped toss the salad. The table was already set with fine china, candles, and a white lace tablecloth.

Naomi brought out a platter with the rack of lamb surrounded by roasted potatoes, carrots, and small onions swimming in gravy that caught Marcel's attention. Asparagus tips, a big salad, and homemade sourdough bread rounded out the menu.

Naomi handed over a corkscrew and the wine that Marcel had brought. "You can be in charge of this."

"Everything looks fabulous, and smells even better," Marcel said. She poured the wine and hoped her mother's Post-it on the bottle was accurate.

"I remember the first time I saw you," Naomi said as she sat down at the table. "That night we played miniature golf and Cricket's golf ball went sailing across the lagoon. I remember thinking how easily you took control of things, and how surprised I was to hear you speaking German to the man who returned the ball."

"And I remember Cricket flirting with you all evening."

"Well . . . yes. She knew I was nervous about meeting you."

Marcel laughed. "Sure you were."

"Getting back to my point," Naomi said as she passed the bowl of salad, "my grandparents fled Germany just before the war, so hearing German when I was growing up was a huge childhood memory for me. I miss it sometimes. I remembered flashes of those times when I heard you speaking to that man."

Marcel said a few words in German, and Naomi smiled and handed the *salzstreuer* — the salt "sprinkler" — to her as requested.

They spent the next two hours asking each other questions about their families, work, and ex-lovers. Naomi had just come out to her parents and siblings during the last year and hadn't been back to New Jersey to see them since then.

"What made you tell them?" Marcel asked from her comfortable position in the recliner. Naomi was stretched out on the sofa; they both had a little buzz from the wine.

"I'm forty years old," Naomi said. "Nice Jewish girls are all married by now. My family was reaching the point of desperation, and they kept trying to fix me up whenever I went home to see them."

They both laughed, and Naomi shook her head. Marcel liked the way her curls framed her face, and wondered briefly what it would feel like to touch them.

"My father would bring these nice young men home with him whenever I went for a visit," Naomi said. "I'm thinking,

'*Oy*. Another cousin I haven't seen in years,' and then the next thing I know I'm meeting this guy's parents who are *not* my aunt and uncle. And the same thing would happen with my brothers. They'd bring their friends over to meet me, and all I could think to say to them was, 'So. Do you have any unmarried sisters my age?' After a while it just seemed easier to tell them."

Smiling, Marcel asked when her next visit to New Jersey would be.

"I'm waiting for things to settle down a little," Naomi said with a shrug. "Ten, fifteen years maybe." Her light laughter made Marcel chuckle, and Marcel admitted to herself once again how much she liked this woman.

Glancing at her watch, Marcel couldn't believe how late it was already. "Wow," she said and got the recliner into a less comfortable position. "How'd it get to be so late? I'm sure you have to work tomorrow too."

They were both standing now, officially signaling the end of the evening. Marcel picked up her empty wineglass and got her keys off the coffee table. She took her glass to the kitchen and said, "The whole evening was great. You're an excellent cook, by the way. Or did I mention that already?"

They were by the front door now, and Marcel found herself reluctant to leave.

"Lamb stew tomorrow night if you're interested," Naomi said.

Once again Marcel could see the uncertainty in Naomi's eyes. That shyness Marcel remembered from earlier was back again, and it made Marcel want to tell her about having a good time . . . that she liked being with her . . . that everything was okay . . . that she couldn't imagine walking out that door without kissing her. But instead Marcel quietly said, "Lamb stew it is then."

And suddenly she didn't want to leave at all. Going out that door would be impossible at that very moment, and she held her breath as Naomi slowly came toward her and touched Marcel's cheek with the back of her hand.

Marcel leaned in to kiss her, and the soft, electrifying connection eased into a slow pulsating need that made her want more. Naomi's touch was no longer hesitant or uncertain as she moved one hand to the back of Marcel's head.

There was no longer a question about what would happen next. They would make love before the night was over, and Marcel relayed this desire with a deep kiss. Again and again they kissed this way, and Marcel inhaled the intoxicating scent of Naomi's perfume. She loved the taste of wine on her lips, and when Naomi took Marcel's tongue into her mouth, Marcel's soft moan emphasized how much they both wanted this.

After what seemed like only a few minutes, Naomi pulled away and took Marcel by the hand, leading her down a hall to a bedroom. Once they were there, the momentum changed, and Naomi was like a finely tuned machine that moved with purpose and precision. She removed Marcel's clothes as though each button's undoing had been choreographed. There was no fumbling or frustration at the amount of time it took, and with each new bit of Marcel's body that was revealed and exposed, Naomi's warm mouth was there to welcome it.

Marcel was trembling. She wasn't sure what she wanted more — to kiss her again or be kissed by her again. Either way Marcel had to have those exquisite lips once more, had to lose herself in this woman's touch.

Nude and radiant, Naomi threw the covers back and slipped into bed. She held her hand out and pulled Marcel down to her. As Naomi wrapped her arms around her, Marcel could feel herself melting into the warmth and softness of Naomi's body. Marcel kissed her over and over again and crushed those marvelous curls with both hands as Naomi rolled on top of her.

No words were spoken; none had to be. Marcel saw the

desire in Naomi's eyes and knew it matched her own. Naomi leaned down and touched her tongue to a nipple and asked Marcel if her breasts were tender.

"No," Marcel said. She wanted more, more of whatever it was that Naomi was doing.

Chapter Seventeen

Marcel drifted as Naomi lay in her arms. Naomi's tongue lightly traced Marcel's left nipple, and occasionally she would take it between her lips and suck ever so slightly. An electric current scampered through Marcel's body each time Naomi did that.

Marcel felt so different from the way she usually did after making love. The tension that usually kept her awake was absent. And now here she was in Naomi's bed, holding Naomi in her arms, feeling aroused all over again by those soft lips teasing her nipples. Naomi had already made love to her once and had caused Marcel's toes to curl in a way she hadn't experienced before. And then when Marcel had rolled Naomi over on her back, Marcel discovered how much Naomi liked having her on top, and a nice rocking-grinding dance developed before they finally came together in a burst of sensation.

"Can I touch you again?" Naomi whispered a while later. Her lips returned to Marcel's nipple, and she didn't wait for a reply as her hand moved down Marcel's body. The featherlike stroking began, and Marcel forgot where she was, who she was, what she was doing, or what was being done to her. There was only the drifting and a semiconscious floating as Naomi continued playing with her and gently opening her up for further exploration.

"Is this okay?" Naomi asked softly.

"Yes," Marcel replied in a breathy whisper. "God, yes."

Naomi propped herself up on an elbow but kept her fingers busy with a slow, steady circling motion. "The first night I saw you I imagined doing this to you." She leaned closer and traced the tip of her tongue lightly around Marcel's ear. Her tongue lightly darted along the outside of Marcel's earlobe before she said, "I want to taste you, baby. Right now. Would that be okay?"

Marcel moaned and felt her body tremble.

"I want my mouth on you," Naomi whispered. "Right here. Right now."

"Yes," Marcel said, as her breathing became ragged.

"I'll make long, slow strokes with my tongue," Naomi said softly. "And then I'll take your clit in my mouth like this," she whispered just before sucking Marcel's earlobe into her warm, wet mouth. Marcel was seconds away from coming and didn't want anything to stop what was happening. She turned her head and found Naomi's mouth and kissed her deeply as her body shuddered with orgasm. Naomi's fingers seemed to know just the right amount of pressure Marcel needed then, and she seemed to know when to stop and hold her there. Marcel was exhausted but smiling; she felt so loved at that moment that she thought she might cry. Marcel hugged her, and Naomi covered Marcel's face with tiny kisses.

"But darling," Naomi said as Marcel kissed her again on the lips. "You came before I got there."

"That was incredible," Marcel managed to say.

Naomi slowly removed her fingers and caressed the inside of Marcel's thigh. "I want your body to know me and remember me."

"That won't be a problem," Marcel said dreamily. "It's thanking you right now as we speak."

Marcel didn't know when the touching eventually stopped. All she remembered was drifting again and feeling safe and content. A while later, a loud noise made her turn over once, but other than that, she didn't remember anything else.

"Hey, you," Naomi whispered as she eased down on the side of the bed. Marcel liked the way Naomi kissed her on the forehead, and she tried opening her eyes.

"What time is it?" Marcel asked sleepily before focusing on Naomi. "Why are you dressed?"

Naomi had on a red-and-yellow flower-print skirt and a yellow cotton blouse. "I didn't have the heart to wake you."

"What time is it?"

"Seven," Naomi said as she briefly swept wayward hair from Marcel's brow. "And I need to get to work."

"Seven in the *morning*?" Marcel said incredulously. She sat up in bed and noticed for the first time that it was daylight outside.

Naomi laughed. "Yes. Seven in the morning. And if I don't leave right now I'll be late." She leaned over and picked up a key from the nightstand. "Keep this and lock up if you leave. But stay as long as you want."

Their eyes met, and Naomi leaned over and kissed her. "As long as you want," she whispered against Marcel's lips.

Marcel felt the beginnings of arousal and kissed her again, only this time she touched Naomi's face and hair.

"Will you come over for dinner tonight?" Naomi whispered breathlessly.

"Will I get more of this?" Marcel asked as she kissed her throat.

"I can guarantee it."

"Then I'll be here."

"Are you okay?" Carmen asked. "You look different, and I'm getting some strange vibes from you."

"I got nine hours of sleep last night."

"*Nine*? Nine hours in a row?"

"In a row. I'm not sure I've had nine hours all month. And I've never had nine in a row without anesthesia."

As Marcel stayed busy with customers that morning, she kept remembering the way Naomi's body felt against hers, the way Naomi seemed to know how to touch her. It had been an incredible night, and Marcel was still processing most of it. *Maybe she drugged me,* Marcel thought with a laugh. *Or maybe lamb makes me sleepy. Instead of counting sheep to go to sleep, maybe I have to eat them instead.*

Later that morning, Roslin called to check on her. "Where were you last night? You didn't come home!"

"I was doing the same thing you were doing the night before."

"Oh." Roslin's laughter made Marcel laugh too. "I bet I had more fun!"

"You forget that I'm the one who taught Cricket

everything she knows," Marcel said. Her mother's silence made Marcel laugh all over again. "Oh, by the way," Marcel added, "I probably won't be home tonight either."

"That makes two of us."

A while later when Naomi arrived with lunch for the three of them, Marcel was so happy to see her that it was all she could do to keep from scooping her up and kissing her right there in the showroom. Marcel took care of the two customers in the shop while Carmen and Naomi chatted and unpacked the feast that Naomi had brought. The smell of chicken salad with alfalfa sprouts on thick homemade bread, as well as lemon-potato soup filled the showroom and even made the customers inquire where they could get the exact same thing.

As soon as the customers were gone, Carmen suggested that Marcel and Naomi have their lunch in Marcel's office while she took care of the store.

"But we've got everything fixed so nicely here," Naomi said, indicating the paper napkins they were using as plates.

Carmen carefully toted a sandwich and a cup of soup into Marcel's office and set it on the desk. Marcel looked at her with a raised eyebrow, but Carmen just nodded toward the other sandwich and soup cup and said, "Your office."

Naomi picked up the sandwich and Marcel took the soup, and they went into Marcel's office like two scolded children. Carmen closed the door, and Marcel immediately felt nervous. The small bed was right there and couldn't have been more obvious had there been neon lights strung around it.

As Marcel stood there holding the warm container of soup, Naomi took it from her and set it on the desk. She then kissed her with such passion that Marcel felt tingly all over. She remembered Naomi's perfume from the night before and earlier that morning; she wanted her touch, her kisses, her boundless energy and enthusiasm.

Before they got to the bed, Marcel's shirt was open and her bra undone. Had there been an Olympic event in ridding someone of their clothing, Naomi Shapiro would have been a gold medalist.

"You feel so good," Naomi whispered and then kissed her again before moving down to concentrate on Marcel's breasts. "So good."

Thank you, dear mother, for insisting on putting this bed in here, Marcel thought fleetingly as she fumbled with the buttons on Naomi's blouse. *Otherwise I'd be doing this on my desk with chicken salad stuck to my butt.*

Marcel kissed her and felt a surge of pleasure as Naomi's tongue touched hers. There was definitely something to be said for making love with one's clothes on because they were both agonizingly desperate for this. Marcel managed to get her hand under Naomi's skirt, over and into pantyhose and lacy undies. Naomi's sudden intake of breath followed by a long heavy sigh changed their direction for a moment. Naomi's undulating hips set the pace, and their kisses became deep and hungry all over again.

When Naomi finally came with a shudder and a delicious moan, Marcel kept her fingers inside of her until Naomi had stopped moving. Marcel kissed her playfully on the nose and cheek, and coaxed a drowsy smile from her. Naomi opened her eyes and seemed to have trouble focusing, but that contented expression Marcel saw made her deliriously happy.

"So good," Naomi whispered as she softly kissed Marcel on the lips. Before Marcel knew what was happening, however, Naomi was on top of her, nudging loose, opened clothing out of the way. The rustling of Naomi's skirt and the faint creaking of the bed as they moved helped fuel this raging fire inside of her. Marcel loved the way Naomi teased her with her mouth, the way she took such care in arousing her. Down she went, farther and farther, kissing Marcel's breasts and stomach. Marcel's pants were unfastened and the zipper eased down. The bed was too small to make this a comfortable adventure for either of them, and Marcel knew that Naomi had to go back to work.

"Come here," Marcel said, and touched Naomi's head. Naomi reluctantly stopped what she was doing as Marcel tugged on her arm and then kissed her as they lay side by side on the small bed.

Naomi was not to be denied, and took control of the kiss, of Marcel's aching body as well as her thumping heart. Marcel felt wild and insatiable as the kiss deepened. Naomi seemed hungry for her, ravenous in many respects, as her hands sought familiar places that secretly begged for attention. Marcel's body screamed for joy when Naomi finally touched her. There was no pretense about how much Marcel wanted this, and Naomi rose to the occasion with a steady stroking.

"You're so wet," Naomi whispered. "God, you're so wet."

A few seconds later, Marcel was already close to the edge when Naomi's tongue touched her left nipple. Marcel came with such intensity that she forgot to breathe as she grabbed Naomi and pulled her close.

When Marcel finally stopped trembling, she was exhausted. Naomi snuggled into her arms and gently kissed her cheek, but kept her fingers inside of Marcel. The light feathery strokes began a bit later, and Marcel remembered how soothing and hypnotic that had been the night before. She drifted to sleep and felt as if she had surrendered to a higher power. All her defenses were down; Marcel was weak and helpless.

After what seemed like only minutes, Naomi kissed her gently on the lips and whispered, "I need to get back to work, baby."

Marcel tried to open her eyes, but they wouldn't function right. She felt Naomi ease away from her and get up from the bed, but Marcel's limbs were heavy. Whatever Naomi was saying didn't make any sense to her.

"I'll see you tonight," Naomi whispered, and then kissed her cheek.

"Wait," Marcel mumbled as she reached for her. "You're leaving?"

"I have to get back to work. I'm teaching a class in twenty minutes."

"Oh."

Naomi chuckled. "Go back to sleep. I'll see you tonight."

Marcel vaguely heard the door open and then close again. *Okay,* she thought as she burrowed deeper into the pillow. Jeez . . . okay . . . okay . . . so . . . so it's definitely not the lamb.

After work Marcel went home, took a shower, and changed clothes. Roslin was in the living room on the phone when Marcel came back downstairs. She still couldn't believe what had happened to her that day. Marcel had slept most of the afternoon, and she hadn't waked up until an hour before closing time. On her desk in her office, she had found two cups of stone-cold potato soup and a chicken salad sandwich on stale bread. When she had finally come out of her office in a groggy state, she remembered how Carmen's knowing grin had managed to embarrass her.

"There you are," Roslin said as Marcel came into the living room. "Where are you off to?"

"I have a date," Marcel said, and then smiled as she thought about adding, *with a woman who makes me sleepy.*

The doorbell rang, and Marcel went to answer it. A well-dressed man in a suit, tie, and Tom Landry hat was there, asking for her by name. When Marcel identified herself, the man served her with the subpoena.

"What now?" Roslin asked as she peered over Marcel's shoulder to get a better look at the document. "Didn't I tell you to let me handle it?"

Marcel went to the phone and called her lawyer; she gave the word to draw up the paperwork to sue the Wheatlys for libel and slander.

~ ~ ~ ~ ~

"I'm starving," Marcel said as she sat down at the table in Naomi's dining room. With a wink she added, "I didn't eat lunch, you know."

"Well, you certainly had the opportunity," Naomi said with a grin.

It was already late, but hunger and the promise of lamb stew got them up a few hours later, and Marcel felt rested and content. She liked Naomi's eagerness to please, as well as her attention to detail in everything she did.

As Marcel dipped out a bowl of stew, she filled Naomi in on the general's lawsuit, the subpoena, and the possibility of some adverse publicity in the future.

"How adverse is adverse?" Naomi asked.

"I don't really know yet. Newspapers seem to like this sort of thing, and since there's a lesbian angle, it could get ugly very quickly."

Naomi sat back in her chair and looked at Marcel with a worried expression before saying, "I can't be out, you know."

Marcel nodded as the realization of what was taking place firmly smacked her up beside the head. Marcel understood better than most the need to keep one's sexual preference a private matter. She had been doing it her whole life, and now it was so ironic that she, Marcel Robicheaux, was the one bringing this threat into someone else's life. She and Cricket had often discussed the similar situations of gay teachers and gay soldiers. The results were the same if their true sexual orientation were ever discovered.

"Newspapers," Naomi said.

"Possibly even tabloids," Marcel added in a devastated whisper. Her lawyer had informed her of all the possibilities on the phone earlier, and it had sent her mother into a babbling rage of I-told-you-so's. As Marcel poked at her steaming lamb stew, she noticed that Naomi was very quiet.

"Tabloids," Naomi finally said.

"Reporters, TV cameras, photographers," Marcel added slowly. She put her fork down and saw the uncertainty and fear in Naomi's eyes. It matched what Marcel was feeling in her heart.

"I can't be out," Naomi said again.

"I understand that." Marcel also understood what was being left unsaid between them right then. Naomi was turning pale and seemed to be in shock. Marcel moved her chair back and stood up. "I seem to have underestimated the impact this would have on things. I'm so very, very sorry."

She went into the bedroom and sat down on the edge of the bed. *How can this be happening to me now,* she thought. *I finally get out of the Army unscathed, but this gay curse still follows me wherever I go. But instead of hurting me, it can end up hurting someone I love.*

As she was finishing getting dressed, Naomi came into the bedroom.

"What are we going to do?" Naomi asked quietly as she eased down on the bed beside her.

"*We* aren't going to do anything," Marcel said simply. "I'm going to countersue and sell antiques." She was close to tears, but she willed herself not to cry as she tied her shoes. Shuddering at the injustice of it all, she wondered why it hadn't occurred to her before that this would be a problem for her new lover who just so happened to be a teacher. It had been so easy to assume that retirement would save her from the witch hunts and the homophobic masses. Marcel realized now that she had failed to see how her life and her actions affected others.

"Please," Naomi said, as she nudged Marcel back on the bed. She slowly crawled on top of her and straddled her body, making that roller-coaster feeling tumble through Marcel's psyche. "Let me ask the same question a different way this time," Naomi whispered as she ran a finger along Marcel's cheek and down her chin. "What are we going to do about this, baby?" The delicate finger continued down Marcel's chin and over the pulse in her throat, lingering at the top of her breasts. "I can't be out," Naomi whispered, "but I won't give you up. So what's our plan?"

Her long, nimble fingers deftly unbuttoned Marcel's shirt again, and Naomi cupped her breast as she leaned down to kiss her. "I won't give you up," she whispered.

"That might be our only option for a while," Marcel said. "You can't be out, and my name and face could become the object of a feeding frenzy."

"We're resourceful women," Naomi said. "That can't be the only answer. I won't let it be the only answer."

A slow session of kissing and touching began, and before long their clothes were twisted and bunched up all around their hot, writhing bodies. Marcel could tell that Naomi was also enjoying the pace, but they eventually wanted more and unceremoniously shed their clothes.

"No way am I giving you up," Naomi said a bit more firmly as she rolled over and pulled Marcel on top of her. "That's out of the question. Totally impossible."

"Then think about us not seeing each other until this thing blows over."

As Naomi kissed her, butterflies fluttered through Marcel's stomach.

"But later," Marcel whispered. "Let's think about it later."

Chapter Eighteen

As Marcel drove home from work Wednesday afternoon, the dark sky and distant thunder that had persistently teased them was the only thing cheering her up. She and Naomi had decided not to see each other again until some of the lawsuit trauma was over with, and the compromise was difficult for them. It had only been three days since they were last together, but it seemed much longer. At one point on Sunday afternoon, Naomi had told her that she no longer cared about the publicity or whatever fallout would result from their being together.

"You're the only thing that matters to me," Naomi had said as they lain in bed Sunday afternoon.

Marcel shook her head. "If this thing goes the way I'm

thinking it could, you'll be glad I'm nowhere near you when it happens. You could lose your job." Marcel kissed her on the end of the nose. "That's not exactly the best way to start a new relationship."

Naomi rubbed the inside of Marcel's bare thigh and slowly brought her hand up until Marcel began to purr. "No matter what happens, lover," Naomi whispered, "I'll be with you through all of it, okay? One way or another."

Once the light stroking began, Marcel had trouble thinking clearly, but afterward she had a chance to address her misgivings again as they drifted off to sleep in each other's arms.

"We'll see how things go with the countersuit," Marcel mumbled. She nuzzled into Naomi's sweet-smelling neck and felt the warm flow of drowsiness begin to take over.

"I'm not giving you up," Naomi said as she kissed the side of Marcel's head.

"We can be in touch by phone. Once a day," Marcel said. "I can't be worried about the Wheatly thing, my business being ruined, and your career and future getting trounced on." With her eyes closed now, the feel of Naomi's soft, warm body next to hers was more relaxing than that kelp concoction Carmen always made her drink.

"Sorry, baby, but one phone call a day just won't cut it for me."

Marcel remembered smiling then and nuzzling deeper into Naomi's body. The next morning, she was able to talk her into taking a break for a few days to see what would happen with the suit that she had filed against the Wheatlys.

"The guy sounds like an idiot," Naomi said. "Isn't he worried about how this looks for him?"

Marcel shrugged. "My lawsuit just might be the thing to wake him up a little." She put her shoes on and leaned back on the bed to watch Naomi finish dressing for work.

"Keep looking at me like that and we'll both be late," Naomi warned as their eyes met in the mirror over the dresser. She worked a little mousse into her hair and then put on earrings.

"I'll call you tonight," Marcel said. The thought of not seeing her for a while was already depressing.

"You're really serious about this separation thing," Naomi said.

Marcel nodded slowly. "If a newspaper outs you, it's like losing your virginity. You can't take it back." She got up from the bed and put her arms around her. In doing so, Marcel instantly wondered where she would find the strength to stay away from her. "Don't think for a minute that this is easy for me."

"I know," Naomi said. "You have enough to worry about without adding me to the list, but how can I make you understand that I'd like to be more than just a thing on a list?" She put her arms around Marcel's neck. "Instead of me being something you have to take care of, maybe I'm the one who can finally take care of you."

Marcel thought about that for a moment; the look on her face made Naomi laugh and kiss her lightly on the lips.

"Surely someone has offered to take care of you before," Naomi said.

"Uh . . . maybe. Uncle Sam did."

With a nice rub on her back, Naomi smiled and said, "Trust me, baby. I'll do a much better job."

And now it was three days later and Marcel had regretted their one-phone-call arrangement many times over already, but in Marcel's mind, the uncertainty of where this "Wheatly thing" was headed made their precautions even that much more important. She had no problem taking the Wheatlys down with her, but there was no way she was going to hurt anyone else over this nonsense. And the more she thought about Jordan and her lies, the angrier Marcel became. She had almost convinced herself that she had made a mistake by not letting her mother handle things. Seeing the General in cement combat boots — and maybe Jordan, too — was sounding more and more like a good idea.

Marcel met her mother coming out of the house, and she felt a little twinge of jealousy at Roslin's good fortune at being able to see her new girlfriend while Marcel was stuck at home with little more than a phone call to keep her warm later.

"Don't wait up for me!" Roslin called as gravel crunched under her feet on her way to her car.

"Wouldn't dream of it," Marcel said.

Once inside she found something to eat in the refrigerator and then went directly to her study and started working. The Antique Villa was once again in need of inventory since business was doing so well, and another buying trip was in Marcel's future within the next few days.

When Naomi called a while later, it took nothing more than the sound of her voice for Marcel's body to begin missing her all over again. It was no longer a surprise to Marcel how eager she was to experience Naomi's touch again. Marcel was also quick to remember how difficult it had been lately for her to fall asleep alone.

"I hate this," Naomi said as soon as Marcel answered the phone. "Please let me come over. I'll scale your fence from the alley and sneak in the back door. I promise no one will see me."

Marcel chuckled. "You'd set off every barking dog in the neighborhood."

"Then I'll disguise myself in that pizza-girl outfit I wore for Halloween." Naomi lowered her voice suggestively. "Are you a good tipper?"

"I have my moments."

There was silence, and then Marcel heard Naomi's deep sigh before she said, "I miss you, baby."

And against her better judgment and everything that seemed right and safe in the world, Marcel asked her how soon she could get there.

~ ~ ~ ~ ~

She answered the door fifteen minutes later, and Naomi was in her arms, kissing her as though it had been months instead of days since they had been together.

"I don't care what happens," Naomi said in between feverish kisses. "I have to be with you."

"I know." Marcel felt complete for the first time since she had left Naomi's bed Monday morning.

"God, you feel good," Naomi said with a little moan.

"Let's go upstairs."

Kissing, kissing, and more kissing kept them glued to each other until their hands began to wander and their breathing became ragged.

"Let's go upstairs," Marcel said again, but neither stopped the kissing long enough to do anything about it. Then somewhere in the distance, Marcel heard slamming car doors and loud voices. There were people in the driveway, and seconds later they were on the porch.

Roslin stormed through the front door and then banged it shut. Marcel and Naomi looked over just in time to see Cricket open the door again. Carmen was right behind her, and all three started talking at once.

"Will you listen to me for a minute?" Cricket yelled.

Both Cricket and Roslin had been crying. Marcel turned to look at Carmen, who was nodding toward the living room; Marcel and Naomi followed her in there.

"What the hell's going on?" Marcel asked as soon as they were far enough away that the other two couldn't hear.

"I don't even know where to begin."

"Why don't you start with why the three of you are together in the first place?"

Cricket came into the room and grabbed Marcel by the hand and pulled her along until they were at the bottom of the stairs. "Go up there and tell her to come down! She won't talk to me."

Marcel retrieved her hand and shook her head. "Not until you get back in there and tell me what happened."

Eventually Cricket calmed down enough to sit, and then Marcel asked Carmen to do all the talking.

"It was your mother's idea," Carmen said, tossing out that disclaimer right away. "We set up a little stakeout across the street from Jordan's new apartment so we could find out for sure who she was seeing. Roslin was convinced that Jordan was involved with more than one woman."

Cricket sniffed and shifted in her chair. "It felt like we were Charlie's Angels or something," Cricket said. "It started out being a lot of fun."

Marcel rolled her eyes and mumbled, "Charlie's Angels. More like Huey, Dewey, and Louie. Or Moe, Curley, and Larry."

"Oh, shut up," Cricket said and then started to cry again. "Please go get her for me. She won't talk to me."

"Not until I know exactly what happened," Marcel said. "If you three have screwed up my case I'll —"

"It's nothing like that," Carmen said, and then looked over at Cricket. "We saw the other woman and got pictures of Jordan kissing her." Then Carmen said simply, "It was Amanda, by the way."

Stunned, Marcel could do nothing but stare. She saw Cricket run from the room.

"Amanda and Jordan," Marcel repeated.

Carmen nodded. "Amanda and Jordan. And apparently it's been going on for quite some time."

"How long?"

"Cricket thinks they slept together the night of your retirement party."

"Are you telling me that Amanda and Jordan were sleeping together when the General found out that Jordan was having a lesbian affair?"

"None of that's been officially confirmed, but that's more or less the idea." Carmen sat on the arm of the sofa and stroked her chin thoughtfully. "My hunch is that Jordan was having flings with Captain Cooper and Amanda at the same time, but whatever it was that the General discovered, it incriminated a woman in the military in some sort of way. Bringing up your name drew the scent away from Heidi and onto you, so to speak." Carmen shrugged. "At least that's my theory."

"What are the chances that Amanda has known what Jordan was up to all along?" Marcel asked. *That would explain the mysterious phone call at the club the night we made love,* Marcel thought. *It must have been Jordan who called Amanda that night.*

"Nothing would surprise me."

Marcel was angry at having been lied to yet again by Amanda and made a fool of by Jordan, but she was also confused about a few other things as well.

"So why is my mother so upset?" Marcel asked. Needing to feel close to Naomi right then, Marcel reached over and took her hand and kissed it.

Carmen let loose with a frustrated sigh. "It was the strangest thing! We're there scoping out Jordan with our binoculars, and then we finally get a good shot of the other woman. I mentioned that it looked like Amanda, and Cricket sort of freaks out on us a little. She gets mad and then your mother starts snipping. All of a sudden I'm in a *very* small car. The next thing I know Roslin peels out of there, and now here we are."

"That's it?"

"That's it."

Cricket came back downstairs and was still crying. She leaned her head on the back of the sofa and pounded her fists against it in frustration. "She won't let me in her room, and she won't talk to me!"

"Get a grip," Marcel snapped. She gave Naomi's hand

another swift kiss and then let go of it before yanking Cricket into the other room by the nape of the neck. "Sit," she said and then pointed to the stairs. Cricket did as she was told.

"The three of you were in the car," Marcel said. "You see that Amanda is there with Jordan. Tell me what happened after that."

Cricket covered her face with her hands and sighed heavily. When she finally took her hands away, her voice was low and husky from crying. "Once it was obvious that Amanda was there with Jordan, I got angry. Things started falling into place, and I was furious." She closed her eyes and fought back more tears. "Roz misunderstood what I was feeling and wouldn't listen to me when I tried to explain it to her."

"Explain it to me so I can explain it to her."

Cricket reached for Marcel's hand and locked on with an iron grasp. "Please fix it. Until I got to know *her* better, I always thought you were the most stubborn person I'd ever met."

"You think I got this way by accident?"

Cricket had a faint smile, but it went away when Marcel said, "You still haven't explained anything yet."

"I was angry at Amanda for being a part of all this crap Jordan has put you through. Amanda knew the accusations were false, but she didn't say anything, and it made me mad." Cricket closed her eyes and sighed again. "So in the meantime, your mother was thinking that I was jealous of Amanda being with Jordan, when that had nothing to do with why I was upset. But she won't listen to me. She's beyond my reach." Cricket sniffed again and visibly tried to pull herself together. "So I need for you to get yourself up there and talk to her for me. And if you get me back in her good graces, I'll forgive you for that other thing you did that pissed me off so bad . . . whatever it was. I don't even remember anymore."

"It would behoove you right now to say please."

"Please."

"Now swear to me that you're telling me the truth and that you're not still hung up on Amanda."

"I'm in love with your mother, Marcel. Please go fix it." She moved over so Marcel could get by on her way up the stairs.

Chapter Nineteen

When her mother opened the bedroom door, Marcel was surprised to find her packing. Marcel stretched out on the foot of Roslin's bed and watched her carefully fold each garment before putting it away in a suitcase. Roslin was still crying, and Marcel was unsure what to do next.

"Where are you off to this time?"

"Vegas."

"What time is your flight?"

"I'll figure that out when I get to the airport."

"Hmm. Okay." Marcel sat up on the bed. "I need a favor," she announced. "This favor will help me sleep while you're away, so it's important." *Cheap shot using the sleep angle to get her attention,* she thought, *but time is a factor right now.*

Roslin stopped working for a moment, and Marcel patted a place beside her on the bed. "Sit down right here and listen to me for a minute."

Roslin reluctantly sat down on the bed and dabbed at a stray tear with a worn, crumpled tissue.

"Cricket," Marcel called. "I know you're there outside the door, so get in here."

The door opened slowly, and Cricket's shaggy red head appeared. Marcel heard her mother sniff again, but she didn't look up. Marcel patted the bed beside Roslin and indicated that Cricket was to sit there. To her mother, Marcel said, "Give her five uninterrupted minutes, and if you still want to go to the airport afterward, then I'll take you as soon as you're ready."

She left and closed the door behind her. Glancing at her watch so she would have an idea how well Cricket was doing, Marcel went downstairs to find Naomi. An emergency hug was on her agenda right then, but Carmen was the only one in the living room.

"Where's Naomi?"

Carmen slipped a CD into the player and turned the music down low. "She left."

"What?" Marcel said, surprised and disappointed since she thought Naomi would be spending the night. "When?"

"Not too long after you went upstairs. Cricket let it slip that you and Amanda had slept together recently. Naomi left right after that."

Marcel felt like someone had slapped her.

"It wasn't a malicious thing," Carmen said. "Just Cricket running her mouth when she shouldn't have."

Marcel looked at her watch again and knew that Naomi couldn't be home yet, so there was no use trying to call her there. She also didn't want to deal with any of this over the phone, so she asked Carmen if she would hang around for a while in case Roslin needed to go to the airport after all.

"Make yourself at home," Marcel said. "You know where everything is." She found her keys and headed for the door.

"Good luck," Carmen called after her.

The wind had picked up a bit, and Marcel could smell rain in the air the moment she stepped out of the house. She locked the door and hurried down the sidewalk to the circle drive where she saw Naomi's car parked. Marcel sighed with relief and slowed her pace. She approached the car, then tapped on the window of the driver's side. Naomi took her time rolling it down.

"Please come back to the house," Marcel said. She had visions of sending Carmen home and then sitting with Naomi in the living room where they would talk this thing through.

"Not yet."

"Then I'm coming in there," Marcel said and went around the car and opened the other door. Light rain began to fall as soon as she got in.

It was dark and much too quiet. Marcel couldn't stand it any longer. She had to touch her and tell her, in the simplest way possible, what she was feeling. She reached over and found Naomi's hand. She knew that things would be okay when Naomi gave hers a squeeze in return.

"I hear that Cricket said something that upset you."

"I didn't know you and Amanda were lovers." Naomi turned and looked out the window; Marcel could tell by her voice that she had been crying. "How long has it been going on?" Naomi asked.

"The night the four of us met for dinner at the Quarry."

Naomi released Marcel's hand and folded her arms across her chest. In a low, trembling whisper she said, "How could you do this to me?" Her voice broke, and a sob escaped from her throat. "How could you keep sleeping with her knowing how I felt about you?"

"We were only together that one night." Marcel tugged on her elbow and made Naomi look at her. "Just that one night. Come here and let me hold you."

"One night."

"Yes, one night. The night we all went to dinner and a movie." All attempts to hug her weren't working, so Marcel let go of her. "Tell me what you've been thinking," she said. "That I've somehow been with both you and Amanda all this time?" With a sigh she added, "I work all day, and I'm with you at night. When do I have time for two lovers?"

"You're the only woman I know with a bed in her office."

Marcel was speechless for a moment. "Uh . . . well . . . yes." *That's probably true*, she thought. *Good point.*

"And I know for a fact that you have women there during the day."

"It was just one night." Marcel didn't know what else to say, but she found herself practically dissolving when Naomi leaned over and kissed her. The heat slowly radiated through her body, and she heard Naomi say again, "Just one night?"

"Yes," Marcel said breathlessly. "Just one night."

Naomi renewed the kiss, and Marcel could feel her toes curling.

"Please come back inside with me," Marcel whispered. She wanted nothing more than to have this woman in her arms again. "Please," Marcel whispered.

They hurried through the rain and went into the house holding hands. A smiling Carmen met them in the foyer and pantomimed wiping sweat from her brow. She left right after that and on her way out suggested that Marcel take the next morning off.

Once Marcel and Naomi were alone again, Marcel said, "Come here," and took her in her arms. Marcel buried her face in Naomi's neck and shoulder and finally felt as if she were home again. "It scared me when Carmen said you had gone." She kissed Naomi's cheek and the tip of her nose. "All kinds of things went through my head."

"That makes two of us."

Marcel hugged her tightly again. "It made me realize how much I love you. I hated the thought of you being upset enough to leave that way."

"When I got in the car I couldn't make myself go anywhere. I'm not sure how long I would have stayed there."

Marcel took her by the hand and led her to the stairs. "Well, just so you know, the bed in my office has only been used once."

"Oh sure. Is this the face of a gullible person?"

As Naomi kissed her again, Marcel thought, *Let the tabloids have their way. Newspapers, magazines, TV, and radio stations. We've spent our last night apart.*

Early the next morning, Marcel woke up to Naomi asleep beside her and the sound of muffled voices in the hallway. *My mother's giggling again,* she thought, and then stretched sleepily against Naomi's soft, naked body. Last night had been incredible, and even now Marcel felt as though she were still glowing from Naomi's touch.

She kissed her on the nose and loved the way Naomi smiled and stretched as she was waking up.

"Good morning, baby," Marcel said.

"What time is it? I can't be late for work." And with a surprise show of alertness, Naomi rolled on top of her and planted kisses everywhere.

"We've got time for several things," Marcel said. "God, you feel good."

189

~ ~ ~ ~ ~ ~

"Can you pass a lie detector test?" Roslin asked Marcel as she filled four cups with decaf coffee and then flipped Cricket's giant pancake on the griddle.

"What kind of question is that?" Marcel asked with a furrowed brow.

"Let's get our women off to work and then we'll talk," Roslin said.

The term *our women* made all four of them laugh. Marcel was amazed at how well she was adjusting to Cricket and her mother being lovers.

Cricket borrowed clothes for work from Marcel; Naomi had brought her clothes the evening before. After showers and a hasty breakfast, the four of them ended up in the foyer kissing and cooing before Naomi and Cricket had to dash off to work and fight the early-morning traffic. When their lovers were gone, Marcel and her mother returned to the kitchen to enjoy more coffee.

"So what's all this talk about a lie detector test?" Marcel asked.

"I'm thinking that you need to take one to prove you didn't sleep with the General's wife. We'll keep making you take it until you pass it. Shouldn't be that hard."

Marcel looked at her incredulously and said, "I could pass one on the first try."

"Oh," Roslin said, and then cackled.

"But why would I want to? What's the point? They don't stand up in court, do they?"

"Who knows? We'll ask that lawyer of yours. In the meantime, I've got something else in mind that'll work, but you need to let me handle things my way."

Marcel's look made Roslin laugh heartily again. "And it has nothing to do with encasing the General in cement or anything like that, okay? How did I raise such a suspicious child?"

"How indeed?"

Marcel and Carmen helped the customer get the solid oak table into the back of his pickup, and he assured them that he had someone to help him with it once he got it home.

"My back always remembers right away how heavy real wood is," Marcel said as she put the tailgate up for him. She heard a car door and looked over to find Heidi Cooper coming toward them. Marcel felt a nostalgic twinge at seeing her in uniform and realized how much she missed the simple things about the Army. The shock of opening her closet door every morning and not finding green uniforms there was finally beginning to subside, and if she could just get over lining her shoes up according to style and color, she would be extremely pleased with herself.

It was good seeing Heidi again, and Marcel asked about several of the people they used to work with. William was in touch with Marcel a few times a week on several office-related matters that hadn't been completed yet. He kept her posted on most of the gossip around the Command as well.

The three of them walked into the shop, and Carmen leaned over and whispered in an amused voice, "We could retire all over again if each of them would just buy something big."

Marcel shook her head and closed the door. "What brings you our way this time of day?" she asked. It was only nine-thirty.

"I need to talk to you," Heidi said, "and I didn't want to do it on the phone."

Carmen left them alone and disappeared into her work

area in the back. Marcel noticed how tense Captain Cooper was, but before Marcel could comment on it Heidi said, "I'm here about Jordan. I just found out what happened."

"I see."

In a low, strained voice, she said Marcel's name and then couldn't say anything else.

"Here," Marcel said, pulling a stool out from behind the counter. "Sit down. It can't be that bad."

"I'm so angry about this that I can't even think."

Marcel found another stool in the corner and pulled it up, too. "You've talked to Jordan recently?"

Heidi nodded.

"What did she say?"

"She told me she lied to him about you, and that she had to do it to protect me." Heidi shook her head in disbelief. "I didn't even know he had confronted her. I feel like such a fool." She successfully blinked back tears and took a deep breath. "She also told me that you two had never . . . had never . . ." Heidi stopped and couldn't finish that sentence either.

"So why are you here?" Marcel asked gently.

"Two reasons," Heidi said with a sniff. "Number one is to apologize for getting you mixed up in this."

"That's Jordan's doing, not yours."

With a slight nod, Heidi thanked her. "And the second reason is to see if there's anything I can do to help."

"I appreciate the offer, but there's no need to get you involved in this if we don't have to."

Heidi finally managed a small smile. "Thanks. I really didn't know about any of this, Marcel. I just got a call from her about an hour ago. She told me everything then."

"Did you learn anything from this experience?"

"Oh yes." Heidi stood up and moved her stool out of the way. "I've learned a lot, but there's still plenty to be worried about. Jordan is even more unpredictable now. There's a chance she'll be going with him to D.C."

"Really? She told you that?"

"Yes. The General knows he'll never get his second star if there's a divorce. The two of them might be trying to work things out."

"Just be careful," Marcel said. "And maybe you should try being more selective who you spend your time with."

"I'm swearing off women. This has been just awful. That should take care of the problem."

Marcel got the call from her mother at about three-thirty that afternoon to meet for dinner at the Old San Francisco Steakhouse.

"The General dropped the lawsuit," Roslin had said, "and we're celebrating. Invite Carmen and bring your girlfriend. And dress up a little. The Senator is buying, okay?"

Fifteen minutes later, Marcel's lawyer called to inform her that General Wheatly had indeed dropped his lawsuit.

"Do we know why?" Marcel asked. She had spent a good ten minutes trying to get in touch with her mother again for more details about what had happened, but Roslin wasn't at home and her cell phone was busy.

"His lawyer wouldn't tell me why."

"Do they understand that if there's one peep about any of this, we're suing him?

"He understands that very clearly now."

Marcel hung up the phone and considered going home to talk to her mother, but two customers came in and she wasn't able to get away. *So I guess I get to hear about it with everyone else tonight,* she thought. *I'm sure my mother is enjoying the hell out of this.*

~ ~ ~ ~ ~

Carmen had a family function to attend and couldn't participate in the celebration, but Roslin, Senator Horatio Wainwright — whom Roslin fondly referred to as Skippy — Naomi, Cricket, and Marcel were there and relieved to have the "Wheatly thing" over with. They had the best table in the house and were getting superb service.

"Marcel, I must say your mother has every reason to be proud of you," Senator Wainwright said. "I remember when we were endorsing you for West Point! And look at you now! Makes me feel old."

"Now, Skippy," Roslin said. "You forget sometimes that you *are* old!"

The laughter flowed easily during cocktails, and when the Senator excused himself from the table to grab a few puffs on his cigar, Cricket was the first to ask Roslin what had happened to convince General Wheatly to drop his lawsuit.

Roslin grinned and began her story. "Skippy arranged for me to meet the General at his lawyer's office where I showed them the pictures that we'd taken of Amanda and Jordan. I refrained from mentioning Captain Cooper's name, being as we had no real proof of her involvement. I also told the General that my daughter was willing to take a lie detector test to prove she had nothing to do with his wife's indiscretions."

Reaching for her wineglass, Roslin took a huge sip and slowly set it back down again. "And, unfortunately, none of that made an impression on him."

Cricket groaned as they all realized that Roslin was playing with them.

"So what *did* change his mind!" Cricket said in exasperation.

"The video Skippy has of the General on all fours getting spanked by some nice madam."

"Oh my goodness!" Naomi said, and then howled with

laughter. Cricket joined in and then leaned over to give Roslin a hug.

Marcel didn't know what to say at first. She was just happy to hear that the lawsuit had been dropped. Now Naomi would be safe and they could see each other again without that complication hanging over them.

"So you blackmailed him," Marcel said, summing it all up for them in four simple words.

"I prefer thinking of it as him having a change of heart."

"It's either him or you," Cricket said reasonably. "Don't start feeling sorry for him." Cricket gave her that squinty look that usually meant *don't screw this up for me.* Marcel decided not to bring up the fact that both she and the General were victims in this.

"Where did Senator Skippy get this video?" Cricket asked.

Everyone at the table laughed.

"His name is Senator Wainwright," Roslin said, correcting her with a chuckle. "Not Senator Skippy."

Marcel smiled. "So where *did* your Senator get this video?"

Roslin picked up her glass again and took another big sip. "I didn't ask and he didn't tell."

Cricket groaned. "Well, I personally think you did an excellent job fixing this mess."

Marcel looked at her mother and nodded. "As always. Thank you."

"And not one little chunk of cement had to be used, dear," Roslin reminded her. "Now answer a question for me."

"Sure," Marcel said.

"You really, really, really never slept with Jordan?"

"Really, really, really," Marcel said with a smile. As Naomi reached over and squeezed her hand, she added one more *really* for good measure.

About the Author

Peggy J. Herring lives in south Texas and is the author of six romance novels previously published by Naiad Press.

Visit
Bella Books
at

www.bellabooks.com